"I don't know who you are."

If Gayle was putting him on, Taylor was going to kill her. Slowly.

"You're not joking?" Taylor ground out each one of the words slowly, giving her every opportunity to recant. Praying she'd take it.

Why were her brothers doing this to her? "Sam, Jake, what's going on here?"

Gayle looked from Sam to Jake, then her eyes came to rest on the stranger. Her brothers had played pranks on her before. But this was going a little bit too far.

Gayle gave each of them as much of a piercing, demanding look as she could muster, under the circumstances. "Jake, Sam, one of you tell me. I want to know. Just who is this man?"

Available in January 2007
from Silhouette Special Edition

Husbands and
Other Strangers

MARIE
FERRARELLA

SILHOUETTE®
SPECIAL EDITION™

*First published in Great Britain 2007
Silhouette Books, Eton House, 18-24 Paradise Road,
Richmond, Surrey TW9 1SR*

© Marie Rydzynski-Ferrarella 2006

*ISBN-13: 978 0 373 24736 3
ISBN-10:0 373 24736 2*

23-0107

*Printed and bound in Spain
by Litografia Rosés S.A., Barcelona*

MARIE FERRARELLA

This *USA TODAY* bestselling and RITA® Award-winning author has written over 140 books for Silhouette, some under the name Marie Nicole. Her romances are beloved by fans worldwide.

To Charlie, and remembering

Chapter One

His hands were gentle, so incredibly gentle. They passed over her body slowly, like a warm spring breeze. The hands of a lover. Caressing her. Stroking her. Making her yearn.

She knew instinctively that they were powerful hands—hands that could have just as easily snapped a neck in two if unrestrained anger had flashed through his veins. Which made it all the more wondrous that he could touch her this way. As if he were worshipping her.

As if he were making love to her with just his hands, just his fingertips.

He *was* making love to her.

A moan slipped from her lips, as if the pleasure that filled her was just too much to contain, to keep captive within the vessel of her body. It overflowed from every pore.

Drenching her.

Drenching him.

And then his hands were no longer blazing a trail along her skin. His lips were there instead, anointing her body. She could feel herself trembling as his mouth, ever so lightly, skimmed along her flesh, following the very same path that his fingers had traced just a moment ago.

A century ago, when time began.

She couldn't see him.

Why couldn't she see him? Why, when every fiber of her being felt him, knew him, wanted him, couldn't she see his face? No matter how she tried, how she turned, she couldn't see him. His identity remained hidden from her view.

Her eyes were open, but she couldn't see. She could only sense him. It was as if something inside of her prevented her from seeing him.

He wasn't a stranger. How could he be? She knew who he was, at least in her soul. Somehow, deep within the secret recesses of her mind, she had always known, that he would be coming for her. Coming *to* her. Whoever he was, he was her soul mate, her intended, the one she had been destined for from the very moment destiny began.

Destined to love until the last sands of time blew away into the dark abyss of eternity.

So if her soul knew him so well, why couldn't she see him?

Gayle Conway strained, trying to turn her head, aching for a chance to get a better view. Any view. Aching to see.

But something was holding her back, restraining her movement. A heavy weight was pressing down on her. And there was such exhaustion consuming her she couldn't breathe. Still, with her last ounce of strength, she struggled against the iron bands on her arms.

A sense of overwhelming loss edged out the pleasure within her, like a blot of ink staining every square inch of the bright, colorful material it had been spilled on, obliterating it.

He was gone.

Gone as if he were nothing more than smoke, as if he hadn't existed at all. But he had. She knew he had. He had been as real as she. Now she was left alone, shackled to a hard bed of loneliness.

The moan that came from her lips this time was devoid of pleasure. It was a keening sound, filled with the sorrow of bereavement and loss.

And then something else cut into it. Another sound, another voice.

Something…someone…

Someone was calling to her. Calling her from this oppressive, weighted darkness she was lost in.

The heaviness began to lift. Hands were on her again. But this time they were not gentle hands. Rough hands, trying to snatch at her consciousness. Trying to bring her back around. She could feel hands rubbing her arms, her legs, coaxing the color, the strength back into them. Back into her.

Gayle tried to listen. To recognize. But the voice calling her name belonged to someone she didn't know. A stranger's voice.

"Gayle, please wake up. Honey, please, just open your eyes. Just look at me. Please."

Fingers. Gentle fingers, not running along her body but lacing her fingers with them. More words.

Supplications? Prayers?

Prayers. Someone was praying over her. She felt more than heard the words, as if they were being whispered into her subconscious.

Gayle tried hard to open her eyes, but they wouldn't move. Each lid felt as if it had been sealed permanently shut.

She *had* to open her eyes to find who'd been loving her. She had to find the man who had so abruptly left her side.

The man she couldn't see.

Slowly, mercifully, she could feel herself rising from the depths, the almost life-threatening heaviness leaving her. A moment longer and it would be all right. She would be out of this lonely, stark world and reunited with the man whose passion had set her on fire. Already she could feel her body warming again. Warming, as if touched by sunlight.

Sunlight.

It was the sun she felt on her face, on her body. The sun. Nothing more, just the sun.

The realization underlined the emptiness in her soul.

Something moist slid from her lashes and slithered in a zigzag pattern along both cheeks. Gayle opened her eyes and looked up at the concerned ring of faces hovering over her.

It took her a moment before she could focus on them. Sam. Jake. The emptiness within her shifted a little as she recognized the familiar faces of her two older brothers.

And then she saw someone else.

Taylor Conway wasn't easily given to allowing his emotions to overtake him, but in the past twenty minutes he had unwillingly sped through an entire gamut of emotions. Every one of them had warred for complete possession of him as he had frantically worked over his wife's body. Equal amounts of CPR and desperation had gone into his attempts to force air into her lungs again. He'd prayed every single prayer he could summon to his numbed brain, making deals with a god he hadn't, until now, known firsthand.

Anything, as long as Gayle came back to him. He couldn't lose her like this. No, not in any way at all. He *refused* to lose her.

Taylor had never tasted real fear before. It was

metallic and bitter on the tongue, worse than anything he'd ever sampled. It had almost choked him.

Just the way the sea had almost choked the very life out of Gayle.

But she was alive. Beneath the green bathing suit top her chest was moving ever so slightly. She was breathing, thank God. Taylor was vaguely aware that at this point, he was into God for plenty, but it didn't matter. Nothing mattered as long as Gayle was alive.

The next moment she was coughing, the water she'd taken in spilling from her nose and mouth. Taylor felt light-headed, giddy and only half-conscious of the hot tears stinging his eyes as what had almost happened began to take hold, getting a death grip on his mind.

Gayle struggled to sit up. He almost smiled. That was his Gayle. A fighter. She didn't have enough sense to lie down. Taylor laid a restraining hand on her shoulder.

"Don't try to get up," His voice threatened to break. Damn, but she had scared the hell out of him.

Taylor quickly looked her over. There was a gash on her forehead just beneath the blond hairline. That would explain why she hadn't come up. She must have hit her head against the side of the boat when she dove off the sloop into the choppy blue water. The gash was still bleeding. The blood trickled down, a few drops mingling with the ring of water that surrounded her body on the deck.

Now that she was safe, he could feel his temper

beginning to rise. But he couldn't shout at her yet, demanding to know what the hell she'd been thinking of to pull a stunt like that. Not when she was still so pale and weak.

So he bit back the hot words as best he could, turning instead toward his brother-in-law.

"Sam, where the hell is that first-aid kit you keep around here?"

Jake was already ahead of both of them. It was his sloop and his invitation that had brought everyone together in the first place.

"Right here." Jake knelt beside Taylor, flipping the lock on the dark-blue box. "What do you need?"

"Something to stop the bleeding for now. That gash looks nasty." Rummaging, Taylor found the last butterfly Band-Aid in the rusted box. He peeled off the wrapper and applied it along with pressure to the cut.

He frowned now. God, but she had scared him. Really scared him. Now that it was over, now that she was lying here on the deck of her brother's sloop, alive and fully conscious, Taylor was aware of his own racing pulse, his own shaken feelings. If he didn't love her so much, he would have wrung her fool neck. He might still do it, just on principle.

Shaken, Jake rose to his feet, the first-aid box in his hands. He pushed it toward Sam. "Right." Sam looked down at his sister dubiously. She still looked really pale. "Is she going to be—"

"I'm okay," Gayle cut in, waving away the concern buzzing around her like a swarm of bees.

Why were they talking about her as if she were in another dimension? She was right here. And she hated being fussed over. At least she thought she hated…yes, she did, she hated having a fuss made over her.

Despite the pounding going on inside of it, her head felt as if it was wrapped in cotton.

Gayle narrowed her eyes as she focused on the man who was rising. "Sam." She said the name that came to her aloud, exploring it. Her vision and the fog about her brain slowly began to clear. Sam was her brother. One of her brothers. Silly that for a moment she hadn't remembered. She could just hear what he'd have to say to that if he knew. They both teased her unmercifully as it was.

Sam quickly dropped back to his knees beside her. "What is it, Gayle?"

"Nothing." It took effort to talk. Her throat felt incredibly raw, as if she'd swallowed then coughed up a seashell. "I just wanted to say your name."

Sam and Jake exchanged looks. That sounded way too subdued for Gayle, but then, she'd never almost drowned before. Of the three of them, it was Gayle, the youngest and most agile, who could swim like a fish. Gayle on whom their father had pinned all his hopes from the very beginning.

Gayle took a deep breath. It was cut off by a sharp pain in her lungs. Jackknifing up, she began coughing violently. Half the ocean was still sloshing around inside her. Without being fully conscious of who she grabbed, she clutched at a strong arm, leaning against it as the cough racked her.

"Easy." The same strong hands held her. The hands that had pressed her down before, when she'd struggled so hard to discover the identity of the man who was fading away. The man who'd made love to her. "Don't try to get up just yet," the deep voice warned her. "We don't want you falling over and hitting your head again. I know it's hard, but even your head has a breaking point."

The familiarity and humor veiled an undercurrent of concern. She tried to smile at the words and succeeded only marginally.

"She's not biting your head off. She must have done more damage to her head than we thought," Jake murmured, then went back to the wheel.

Gayle turned her head and winced as pain accompanied the simple movement. "What happened?" she asked Sam. "What am I doing here?"

"I fished you out," Taylor answered. "You insisted on diving off the bow of the sloop." He pointed to where they'd all watched her dive off. It had been on a stupid dare. Taylor had raced over to stop her, but it was too late. "Probably just to annoy me."

When he'd looked down in time to see her slice cleanly into the water, he'd felt his temper rising at her defiance. But it was admittedly mingled with admiration. He couldn't help it. The sight of her form affected him that way. She'd always moved like sheer poetry.

At first when she didn't emerge, he was sure she was doing it just to get back at him for that disagreement they'd had yesterday. Taylor knew she could hold her breath underwater for an inordinate amount of time. Her father, Colonel Lars Elliott, retired, an Olympic gold medalist, had thrown all three of his children into the water long before they could walk, determined to make serious Olympic contenders out of them, just as his father had made of him. More than that, he'd demanded winners. Gayle had been his winner.

But thirty seconds after her dive today, an uneasiness had taken hold of Taylor. Even as Jake and Sam quickly checked the perimeter of the sloop to see if Gayle had come up somewhere away from them, Taylor was diving in to find her. Something told him this wasn't one of the pranks she was so fond of pulling. This was on the level.

He almost hadn't found her. By the time he'd brought her up to the surface, it had been at the last possible moment for him. His lungs had been bursting, screaming for air. He could have made it up faster without her, but he would rather have died with her than let Gayle go and risk anything happening to her.

She blinked, her eyes stinging as she looked at the man beside her in wonder. What he said didn't make sense. "Why would I want to annoy you?"

Taylor rose to his feet, looking down at her. He shook his head and smiled once more. "That's something I ask myself a lot. My only conclusion is that annoying me seems to be a hobby of yours."

Gayle frowned as she stared back at him. As if she didn't know what he was talking about. As if she were looking at him for the first time.

The uneasiness returned, though he couldn't put a name to it.

"I think that blow to the head might have finally succeeded in doing something none of us had ever managed to do. Make you docile," Sam elaborated when she turned her sea-blue eyes on him quizzically. At the helm, Jake laughed.

"Fat chance," Gayle said. Pulling her legs to her, she tried to sit up again.

Taylor started to stop her. "I told you to lie back." Why did she always have to be so damn stubborn? If she had a concussion, movement might make it worse. He was prepared to carry her in his arms from the shore to the hospital if he had to. After what he'd just gone through, he'd prefer it that way.

Rather than lie down, Gayle pulled her arm out of his reach. Who the hell did he think he was? "Why should I listen to you?"

A grin slicing his face, Jake shook his head, relief flooding him. "She's ba-ack."

Taylor ignored him. His eyes were on Gayle's. "Because I'm making sense. Now lie back, damn it." He glanced at the butterfly Band-Aid on her forehead and saw a small, angry red line forming beneath it. "You're still bleeding." He looked over his shoulder at his brother-in-law at the helm. "Jake, can't you make this thing go any faster?"

The waters were getting choppier. The storm was coming sooner than they'd expected. Jake was already pushing the engine to the limit. "I'm trying," Jake answered. Frustration outlined his voice. "This isn't a speedboat."

"Try harder," Taylor snapped. Though he didn't often lose his temper with people other than Gayle, the near tragedy they had narrowly avoided had turned his patience to the consistency of dried kindling. His temper flared easily.

Gayle rallied, taking immediate offense. "Hey, stop yelling at my brothers. Just who the hell are you, anyway?"

"What?" Taylor looked at her incredulously. Now what was she trying to pull?

The question unsettled her a little as she tried to ignore the vague, irritating feeling that she should know the answer to her own question. Gayle licked her lips, tilting her chin slightly.

"I said, who are you?"

Taylor sank down again, his eyes fixed on her face. "What do you mean, who am I?"

Was he deaf as well as belligerent? "Just what I said." Gayle slowly repeated the question. "Who are you? Are you a friend of Sam's?"

He has no idea what kind of a game she was playing, but because she'd just given him the worst scare of his life, and because he still felt a little shell-shocked, he momentarily played along.

"Yes, I'm a friend of Sam's. And a friend of Jake's, too," he added for good measure.

The answer made Gayle frown. She thought she knew most of her brothers' friends. Certainly the ones they had in common. It was what made them such a close-knit family. But she had absolutely no recollection of the brooding, dark-haired man who seemed to think it his God-given duty to order everyone around.

The ache in her head grew even as she tried to ignore it. Gayle peered at his face, searching for some sort of recollection. "Then why have I never met you before?"

Hands on the wheel, Jake turned around. He and Sam exchanged looks. Their unspoken question mirrored each other.

What the hell was Gayle up to this time?

Taylor sat back on his heels, studying Gayle's face. A face he'd long since memorized, every nuance, every fiber. All deeply embedded in his brain.

"Oh, we've met, all right." The deep voice was pregnant with meaning.

Gayle shook off the almost hypnotic effect. Met? She sincerely doubted it. She would have remembered a face like that, even if she'd only seen it just in passing: chiseled, stern, perhaps even hard, to the undiscerning eye; an odd collection of planes and angles that somehow arranged themselves to make the man impossibly handsome.

The total is greater than the sum of the parts, the vague thought echoed through her throbbing head.

But handsome or not, that didn't give him a right to lie to her or play a trick at her expense, especially when her brain felt as if it was the consistency of Swiss cheese.

"No, we haven't met," she insisted stubbornly.

Maybe some other time, when his nerves hadn't been pulled thinner than the thread used for suturing an internal wound, Taylor would have been willing to play along a little longer. But not now. Not when he'd been to hell and back in what could have been a watery grave for both of them. He wasn't in the mood for it.

He reached out to touch her shoulder. "Gayle, I don't feel like playing games."

She shrugged him off again. What made him think he could just touch her like that? As if he had a right to? Why weren't her brothers protesting?

Weakness passed over her, bringing with it a volley of heat that drenched her in perspiration. Gayle would have drawn herself into a ball if she could, locking out everything. For a moment she had to struggle just to hang on to consciousness again. But she refused to surrender.

Gayle gritted her teeth together against it, against the probing fingers of pain.

"Good, because neither do I." Her eyes became dark penetrating slits of blue green as she looked at this man pushing his way into her life. "My head feels like it's coming apart." She held it as if she were afraid that it would. "So, are you going to tell me your name or not?"

Concern returned like a clap of thunder. Sam sat down in front of his sister. He fanned out the fingers of one hand before her face, ignoring her question to Taylor. "Gayle, how many fingers am I holding up now?"

The sharp headache sapped any patience she might have had to spare.

"Three." Gayle closed her hand over Sam's and pushed it aside. "We all know it's as high as you can count. I don't want to play count-the-fingers with you, Sam. I want someone to tell me who this man is and why he's trying to boss everyone around."

Despite the tension in the air, his sister's comment made Jake laugh. "Talk about the pot calling the kettle black." His dark eyes darted toward his brother-in-law. Taylor's face did look pretty strained. Both he and Sam had often marveled how Taylor could have lived with their sister for the past eighteen months and still remained sane. "Not that I mean to imply you're a kettle…" His voice trailed off, having nowhere to go.

Fear began to rear its head again, bringing with it an uneasiness that nibbled away at Taylor. Jake's comment didn't even register. Taylor stared at Gayle, at the woman he had ultimately loved more than the allure of the free life he had abandoned for her.

"You don't know who I am." It sounded absurd

even to say out loud. After what they had shared, he would have said that the pyramids would have become mounds of sand and blown away before she forgot him, or he her. This had to be some kind of game, a cruel prank to get back at him for the argument and God only knew what.

"Yes," Gayle replied. But before he breathed a sigh of relief in misunderstanding, her next words took it away from him—and cleared up the minor confusion while ushering in a complete new truckload. "I don't know who you are."

If she was putting him on, he was going to kill her. Slowly.

"You're not kidding?" He ground out each one of the words slowly, giving her every opportunity to recant. Praying she'd take it.

Because something deep inside her was suddenly afraid, afraid of what she couldn't begin to understand, Gayle clung to temper.

"I'm bleeding. Why would I be kidding?" Why were her brothers doing this to her? Why were they putting her through this charade at a time like this? She looked from one to the other, silently asking them to stop. "Sam, Jake, what's going on here? And how did I get here, on the boat, anyway?"

The three men looked at one another, not knowing whether they were all victims of an elaborate hoax and being played for fools—Gayle wasn't above that—or if they should be seriously worried.

Gayle drew herself up to her knees, swaying just

a little. "I said, what's going on here?" She glanced from Sam to Jake, then her eyes came to rest on the stranger. Her brothers had played pranks on her before. It was a way of letting off steam that was a holdover from their childhood, when their father's rigorous training would get to them. But this was going a little bit too far now.

"Jake, Sam, one of you tell me. I want to know. Just who is this man?"

Chapter Two

Jake was the oldest, and as such, he was apt to take things more seriously than his siblings. He looked at the woman he was fond of calling his baby sister, although it was not quite six years that separated them. There were times when Gayle had trouble knowing when to stop. He had no problem stepping in when it came to that.

"Okay, Gayle, quit fooling around now. You've had your joke and scared the hell out of the rest of us, including your husband."

All she heard was one word. One frightening word. Was she going crazy? Or were they? Knowing her brothers, it was them. And she didn't appreciate being the butt of the joke.

"Husband." Gayle looked around angrily, deliberately *not* focusing on the stranger at her left. "*What* husband?" she demanded.

"That's enough, Gayle." Jake was using his police-detective voice. It masked his growing uneasiness. Gayle wasn't normally such a good actress.

"My sentiments exactly," she retorted, getting to her feet. The pounding in her head increased twofold, ushering in a dizziness that threatened to make her pass out. She mentally clung to her surroundings as she sank onto one of the four seats on the deck. "Now quit fooling around, guys." She put her hand to her head, as if that could somehow contain the headache that was consuming her. "I don't feel right."

Doggedly refusing to step back, Taylor took a closer look at the woman who had been the bane of his existence as well as the center of his universe for the last eighteen months.

What he saw worried him.

He wasn't comfortable in this frame of mind. Marriage had never been in the cards for him as far as he was concerned. Never close to either of his parents, he hadn't wanted a family of his own.

Independent, handy, Taylor had stubbornly made his own way ever since he'd graduated from high school. He returned to college only when he felt that it might give him a leg up in the field that he'd finally chosen for himself: restoring, recreating or just plain overhauling houses that had long since seen their zenith. He took sows' ears and albatrosses, turning them into things of modern beauty and functionality.

Blessed with vision, Taylor considered himself both a craftsman and an artist with a keen eye for detail. He liked working with his hands as well as his mind. Liked partying hard, too, when the occasion called for it. And always, always moving on whenever the next project called. Moving on alone.

Until he'd met Gayle Elliott.

It was, appropriately enough, at a party thrown by Rico Cimmaron, a professional football player. The party was at Rico's house, a building Taylor had renovated for a sinfully exorbitant amount of money. Rico had said as much when he'd introduced him to the small, slender and incredibly sexy woman he was currently dating.

Looking back, Taylor thought everyone should have a moment where the rest of the world faded away as the focus zoomed in on one perfect individual. The way he found himself focusing on Rico's date. Gayle Elliott. He quickly discovered that the golden blonde with the sea-green eyes had an attitude that both pushed him away and reeled him in. By the end of the party, he knew that Gayle was funny, outgoing, witty and as combative as hell when she thought she was right.

He also quickly saw that she was accustomed to being the center of attention, just like Rico. For all intents and purposes, they looked like a golden couple. He didn't let that stand in his way.

Like Rico, she was a name in the world of sports. His knowledge of that world was cursory, but someone at the party obligingly filled him in about Gayle. She'd earned not one but nine gold medals over the course of the last three Summer Olympics, winning her first gold medal at the age of sixteen. After she'd announced her retirement at the close of the Olympic Games, Gayle turned her attention and all her incredible energy and exuberance to sports commentating.

Her enthusiasm for all sports made her a natural. So did her looks. She quickly found herself courted by a number of local news stations around the country. She chose to remain in Bedford because it was her hometown and took the offer from a Los Angeles affiliated station.

Ratings went up and her temporary stint turned into a permanent spot. John Alvarez, the man she'd subbed for, found himself moved to the morning broadcast.

It was to Gayle's credit that Alvarez bore her no resentment. Taylor saw that men of all ages fell all over themselves in their attempt to be around Gayle and garner her favor. Which was precisely why he'd initially held back. That and because she was dating a former client.

He realized his reticence was what had attracted her to him in the first place. In his estimation, the pert, sassy and somewhat opinionated woman wanted to leave no man unconquered. He admitted to Sam, although not to her, that Gayle won him over fast enough. And it was difficult to keep his feelings to himself.

They'd had one hell of a courtship. He liked to think of it as two forces of nature coming together. There was no other explanation why a five-foot-three woman had suddenly taken such a dominant position in his life, when, from an early age on, he'd had his pick of any woman he wanted and had wanted none for the duration.

The way he'd wanted Gayle.

From the very beginning Gayle had turned his life upside down.

And had nearly brought it to a screeching stop just now, when he'd believed for several horrible moments that the waters through which she'd always negotiated her way like a mermaid had suddenly and finally claimed her.

His nerves were stretched to the very limit. Crouching beside her chair, Taylor took hold of his wife's shoulders, pinning her against the teak back. Anger flashed across her face as she attempted to shrug him off. And failed.

She was weak, Taylor thought with concern. If she wasn't, Gayle could have easily worked her way out of his grasp. She had an exorbitant amount of upper body strength.

"You don't remember me," he said, stunned by her statement.

What if it was true? a nagging voice whispered

inside his head. What if, for some awful reason, she couldn't remember him?

Gayle exhaled a ragged breath. What was going on here? And why did she feel as if someone had just shot holes through her every thought? She couldn't remember how she got to this deck. Or even to Sam's boat. She tried to think back to the last thing she could clearly remember. Everything felt murky in her head, as if it was submerged in a tank overgrown with algae.

Panic fueled impatience. She stared at the man crowding her. "No, I don't remember you. Why would I lie?" she demanded.

"Because you're good at it. Not lying," Taylor amended, "just at being stubborn. At playing pranks. And being a pain in the butt," he added, his own temper just about snapping. One minute he was afraid she was dead, now she was pretending not to recognize him. His emotions couldn't handle this uneven roller-coaster ride. "This isn't funny, Gayle."

Anger was her only defense. Her face was deadly serious as she looked at this stranger who was intruding into her life with lead-soled combat boots.

"No," Gayle agreed vehemently, "it's not." She looked to her brothers for help. Why were they humoring this character? Why weren't they coming to her defense? Fun was fun, but this was beginning to be cruel.

"Gayle, you've had your fun—" Sam began, only to be waved back into silence by Taylor.

"I've known her to get pretty elaborate with her jokes, but even Gayle couldn't fake that kind of pallor," he pointed out.

She looked as white as a sheet, he thought with mounting anxiety. And there was something in her eyes that had him coming to the unwelcome realization that his wife *wasn't* kidding around.

She *didn't* remember him.

Moving closer, Jake looked at his brother-in-law. "You think she might have amnesia?"

Taylor rose to his feet. Before he could reply, Sam snorted in disgust. "Amnesia," he repeated, scoffing at the notion. "You don't just forget one person if you have amnesia. It's not selective."

Gayle tugged on the leg of Sam's bathing suit. "Hey, guys, I'm right here. Don't talk about me as if I were some inanimate object."

Her tone was angry, but inside she was beginning to give way to fear. A large, overwhelming, all-encompassing fear because this was beginning to feel strange.

What made matters worse, tipping the scales in Sam and Jake's favor, was that her brain really did feel as if there were holes running all through it.

She clenched her hands in her lap. No, not possible, she thought. Things like this didn't happen. Not to her. Okay, so she couldn't remember the events of this morning. Couldn't remember how she came to be here, but those were just a few random events. And there were all those facts and figures crowding her brain. It was only natural to forget a few things along the way.

Besides, Sam was right. You didn't just forget a whole person, at least not a significant one and husbands definitely came under the heading of significant people. How could she forget a husband and nothing else?

This *had* to be a prank. And once she got them to admit it, she was going to make them all pay for it. Sam and Jake and especially the man with the superserious expression.

"We need to take her to the E.R.," the man was now saying to her brothers, talking again as if she had no more mind than the red cushion against the chair. But at least he was making sense. It was the first thing out of his mouth she agreed with. A doctor would take care of the cut on her forehead, give her something for this awful headache and tell these bozos to quit yanking her chain like this.

"Boat's already turned around," Sam assured him. The next moment he returned to the helm and the wheel he'd left on automatic pilot.

"Good," Gayle declared in a voice she prayed didn't sound as shaky as she felt. "The faster we get this squared away, the better." With superhuman will, she forced herself up to her feet again, then mentally defied that woozy feeling to return. For the moment it seemed to remain at bay, hovering just outside the perimeters of her consciousness.

Her hands clenched at her sides, perspiration

forming along her forehead, she managed to edge closer to Jake. She glanced back toward her so-called "husband" and saw that the man had taken out a cell phone from somewhere. Suspicion rose immediately. She didn't trust this guy any further than she could throw him.

"Who are you calling?" she wanted to know.

"Dr. Peter Sullivan. He's a neurosurgeon at Blair Memorial Hospital."

Her eyes widened. Without realizing it, she took a step closer to Jake. "I'm not letting anyone operate on me."

Finished, Taylor closed the cell phone. He was aware that both her brothers seemed really concerned now. That made three of them. He did his best to keep a poker face. One of them had to look as if they weren't playing pattycake with panic.

"It's not about an operation," he told her. As he took a step closer to her, he noticed her flinch. She didn't even seem to be aware of it. Her involuntary action ate away at his soul. "He's the best in the area." Which, he added silently, considering that the area was Southern California, a region of the country generally thought to be overloaded with doctors from every field of specialization imaginable, was saying a great deal.

Her eyes met his. He saw a familiar look of bravado there. It gave him a measure of hope, even if it was getting in his way at the moment. "Or he's a friend, willing to go along with whatever you tell him to say," she countered.

Her sense of paranoia was still intact, Taylor thought. Over the course of their courtship and marriage, Gayle had always been prepared for another retaliation. He was always careful to choose his paybacks wisely. They fought well and made love even better. Lord, he hadn't known he could feel this happy, this fulfilled until he'd met Gayle.

A cold shiver slithered down his spine. He tried his best to ignore it. She was going to be fine. If this was on the level, she was going to be fine.

If this wasn't, the woman was dead meat.

"We'll be there with you," Jake assured his sister.

Gayle turned to look at him and he saw the fear in her eyes.

So did Taylor. He tried to ignore the sick feeling in the pit of his stomach.

Like Rico, Taylor had met Dr. Sullivan while doing renovations on the man's house just after the surgeon had gotten married. The wedding had made the society page as well as the business section, because the bride was the head of a well-known fashion design company and, along with her younger brother, the owner of the Fortune 500 company that produced the designs.

He saw the man frowning now as he approached him and his brothers-in-law. They'd been cooling their heels in the waiting room, trying to convince one another that this was nothing more than a stupid joke. Getting nowhere.

Peter wore the expression of a man who knew he was not the bearer of good tidings. "The good news is that she checks out fine physically and she can go home."

"And the bad news?" Taylor pressed.

"The bad news," Peter told them, trying to phrase it as clinically, as painlessly as possible, "is that Gayle appears to have sustained a blow to the head and while there doesn't seem to be any evidence of a concussion, it has apparently triggered a bout of amnesia."

"A bout," Taylor repeated. Fighters had bouts. They were over after a given amount of rounds. A bout with the flu lasted a while, then was over. He rallied around the word. "Which means that it'll go away." Taylor silently willed the surgeon to confirm his conclusion.

Peter took a breath, then said, "Probably."

"When?" Taylor pressed before either of his brothers-in-law were able to say the word.

Peter shook his head. He sympathized with what he knew the three men had to be going through, especially Taylor. "I'm afraid that I can't really say. Amnesia is still a very gray area for us."

Taylor felt as if he was free-falling through space, with a terrain full of nothing but jagged rocks beneath him.

"'Appears,' 'apparently,' 'probably,'" he echoed in protest. "There's nothing definite here, Doc."

"No," Peter agreed, "there's not. Amnesia is such

a capricious condition. There are no hard-and-fast rules established yet. This could go away in an hour, a day, a month or…" He let his voice trail off, not wanting to utter the word that he knew Gayle's husband dreaded.

Never.

"Capricious." Jake seized on the doctor's description. "That makes it sound like it's all a prank."

Peter slowly moved his head from side to side. "I'm afraid not."

Taylor had worn a path in the carpet, waiting for the neurosurgeon to emerge. He had to hold himself in check now to keep from pacing again. This just didn't make any sense to him.

"But Gayle can't just forget one thing and not everything else," he protested. And then that sick, sinking feeling had him adding, "Can she?"

"I know it sounds crazy," Peter agreed, "but I'm afraid that she can."

"Selective amnesia?" Taylor scoffed at the notion even as he fought to keep the panic he felt from crawling up his belly and into his throat. "How is that even possible?"

"More easily than you think, Taylor. Actually, all amnesia is selective in a way. A person with amnesia doesn't forget how to talk. How to walk. How to get dressed. They remember who's president or how to make change. They forget other things, things like who they are."

"Okay, she knows all that. She just claims not to know who I am," Taylor bit off, frustrated.

"Has she been taking any new medications?" Peter asked, looking at all three men.

"No. She's as healthy as a horse," Taylor told him. "Why?"

"There was this man, a former astronaut actually, who forgot who his wife was. They thought it was the onset of Alzheimer's, but it was a bad reaction to a statin medication he was taking for his cholesterol. It happens."

"She's not taking anything for cholesterol." Taylor took a second to collect himself. "So what you're saying is that it's possible to forget just one integral part of her life. Me."

"Yes, it's possible."

"Why?" Taylor demanded. He hated this helpless feeling that was taking over. He was a doer, not someone who just sat back to wait. Waiting had never been very popular with him. "Why would Gayle just forget me and not her brothers?"

"I don't have the answer to that," Peter told him honestly.

"Take a guess." It was a barely suppressed plea.

Peter blew out a breath. "There might be some sort of underlying reason. The mind is still largely a huge mystery to us. It represses certain memories, sometimes so much so that the person forgets they ever had them. Gayle hitting her head triggered a response, allowing her mind to spring into action."

"And erase me." The words tasted bitter in Taylor's mouth.

Peter frowned slightly. "I wouldn't have put it exactly that way, but yes, erase you."

Taylor still needed a reason, something to rectify, to make right. "But why?" He looked at Jake and Sam. Along with concern, there was pity in their eyes. He hated being on the receiving end of pity. His frustration continued to mount. "There's nothing wrong between us."

"No explosive events in the past few months?" Peter addressed the question not only to Taylor, but to Gayle's brothers, as well.

"Gayle is always explosive. She's a hotbed of emotion," Sam told him. "She always has been."

"But there hasn't been anything out of the ordinary," Taylor insisted.

It wasn't strictly true. There'd been one argument, a minor one really, especially when you took into consideration that it had been with Gayle. She was usually far more vocal than she had been over this last thing. They'd had a difference of opinion over her getting pregnant. He wanted to wait, and she seemed intent on it happening soon. The reasons for his side were purely logical and perhaps a little chauvinistic.

He wanted to save a little more money before they started a family. Through her endorsements as well as her job, they were far from hurting financially, but he thought of it as "her" money. A baby should be raised with money that *he* provided. He'd said as much and she'd backed away from her position quickly enough. But she hadn't seemed happy about it.

The matter hadn't come up again, so he just thought it was one of those things Gayle occasionally raised, getting on the opposing side of an argument just to goad him. It really hadn't been much of a disagreement as far as some of their disagreements went. He figured she was just testing the waters to see how he felt. Quite honestly, he'd been rather surprised that the discussion had evaporated so quickly.

Taylor tried to think of something else, something remotely major that might have upset her. He came up empty. That couldn't be it.

Shrugging, he said, "She wanted us to go and visit my parents, but I told her I was too busy and she got a little bent out of shape over that. But you're not going to tell me that my wife just suddenly decided to wipe me out of her memory banks because I wouldn't take her for a visit to see her in-laws." He shoved his hands into his pockets. "They're not the kind of people you'd put yourself out for." They weren't even the kind of people you'd bother crossing the street to meet, he added silently, then shook his head. "This can't be about that."

"Whatever it is about, for some reason her mind decided to shut down when it came to things about you. I'm not even sure if anything traumatic is really directly at the heart of this."

He felt they were going around in circles. And he was getting dizzy, as well as despondent, because he was beginning to believe Peter. "But you are sure that Gayle doesn't remember me. That this isn't some elaborate trick."

The doctor's expression told him as much.

Taylor's heart sank even lower.

"There's actually a precedent for this," Peter told him. "There was case several years ago where a woman was involved in an accident. She hit her head and when she came to, she couldn't remember her husband. But she could remember everything else."

Taylor was almost afraid to ask. "Did she ever get over it?"

"Yes." The doctor smiled.

Hope began to rebuild inside of him. "Then it'll be okay."

"Every case is different."

Taylor snorted. "You don't exactly dip into the well of optimism, do you?"

Peter laid his hand on Taylor's shoulder. "Most likely she will come around."

Most likely. He wanted guarantees, not nebulous words he couldn't bank on. "What do I do until then?"

Peter gave him an encouraging smile before he left to see his patient. "Be nice to her."

Chapter Three

"'Be nice to her?'" Sam repeated in disbelief, looking at Taylor once Dr. Sullivan had left. "That's his professional advice to you? 'Be nice to her'?" Stunned almost beyond words, Sam could only shake his head. "Damn it, Taylor, where did you find this guy? In an ad on the back of a comic book?"

"No," Taylor replied slowly. "Actually, he's pretty high up in his field. The guy works miracles."

Even as he spoke, he felt as if the words were bouncing around in an echo chamber in his head. As if nothing around him was real.

This couldn't be happening.

He and Gayle had had a rocky eighteen months,

but they were learning to work things out, to travel on the same road because they loved each other. No matter how heated things got between them, there was always that to fall back on, the love they felt for each other.

And now he was supposed to accept the fact that he was standing out there, alone? That he loved her but she didn't love him because she didn't even know him from any other stranger on the street? How the hell was he supposed to come to terms with that? What did that do to their marriage? To their relationship?

Damn it, he had no frame of reference for this. No idea how to cope.

"Sure doesn't look as if he worked any miracles on Gayle," Sam countered in disgust.

"I think it makes sense," Jake said in his even, quiet voice.

Taylor had to concentrate to keep the fog from closing in around his brain. He looked at Jake and realized he hadn't been listening. That he'd been mentally trying to catch up all the marbles in his hand at once, but they kept insisting on slipping through his fingers and rolling away.

"What does?"

Jake nodded in the general direction that the surgeon had taken. "What the doc said about being nice to Gayle. All you can do is be patient." He put his hand up, forestalling the words he knew had to be coming. "I know it'll be hard, but this condition has *got* to be a temporary thing."

Taylor wished he had Jake's ability to see the bright side of things. But he was a realist who knew that sometimes, the worst could and *did* happen. "And if it's not?"

Jake's small mouth curved ever so slightly, his expression more philosophical than amused. He put his arm around Taylor's shoulders. "Now you see, there's your problem, Taylor. You can't think of this negatively. You've got to believe. Believe that it's going to be all right. Before you know it, Gayle's going to be back to normal." Although the smile remained, there was an enormous depth of feeling behind every word.

"Yeah, and then before you know it, you'll find yourself missing her not knowing you," Sam speculated.

"Yeah," Taylor bit off.

How many times over the course of the last eighteen months, at the height of one of their "disagreements," had he wished he'd never met her? The woman seemed to go out of her way to drive him insane. And yet…

And yet he knew that life before Gayle had been nothing more than an existence, marked by pockets of work he was really proud of and interludes with women that left him feeling empty and somehow lacking. Until Gayle, he hadn't realized exactly what it was that had been lacking. After Gayle came into his life, rolling in like a tempestuous storm, he knew that what had been lacking was color, vibrancy and a zest that had him greeting each day with the enthusiasm of an adventurer poised to take the first step into the greatest adventure of his life.

That was what living with Gayle was like, a constant adventure. Sometimes good, sometimes bad, but always, always stimulating.

There was no way he was going to give that up. No way he was going to give *her* up.

Okay, he thought. This was going to be just another adventure in a long series of adventures. A little strange, but then, life with Gayle had never exactly been what one would call normal.

As long as he kept his eye fixed on the light at the end of the tunnel—as long as he kept telling himself the light was there even when he couldn't see it—he could get through this.

"The doctor said Gayle could go home," Taylor said aloud, more to himself than to Sam and Jake.

Jake nodded, as if to say that this was a good next step. "Then let's go get our girl," he said.

Taylor returned the nod, grateful for his brother-in-law's support. He knew that he could count on both Jake and Sam. Not just because Gayle was their sister, but because he was part of the family. There were times when he caught himself thinking how odd that felt. Eighteen months and he was still adjusting to the idea that he had more than himself to lean on. That he wasn't alone anymore. It was a fringe benefit for getting involved with Gayle.

Flanked by Jake and Sam, Taylor entered the curtained area, ready to pick up the fight where they had left off. Gayle had called him a liar just before the nurse had drawn the curtain around the gurney so that she could change into a hospital gown.

Words melted from his tongue and his head the moment he looked at the woman who no longer remembered that she was his wife. He couldn't recall ever seeing Gayle looking so small, so vulnerable as she did lying in that bed—and yet so defensive at the same time.

She was probably scared. But then, who wouldn't be, in her position? Part of her memory had been whisked away like a so-called alien abduction. That would have rattled anyone. And although she was outgoing, Gayle had never been what he would have called the blindly trusting type.

Which was why she'd been so suspicious of him. Why she was *still* suspicious of him, if that look in her eyes was any indication of the state of her mind.

This was going to take a hell of a lot of patience, he warned himself. More than he'd ever had to dig up before. Taylor really hoped he was up to it.

You *have* to be up to it, he upbraided himself. The prize was far too precious. And he had no intention of losing it.

"The doctor said you could go home now," Taylor told her.

Gayle deliberately looked toward her brothers. The less encouragement she gave this poor joke of theirs, the better. Not that she wouldn't have been interested in spending some time with this guy her brothers had dug up. The man had definite potential, especially around the mouth and eyes.

His dark-blue eyes looked as if they'd been the inspiration that had led someone to coin the phrase about eyes being the windows of the soul. His looked as if they were almost bottomless. And his mouth—there was something incredibly sensual about his mouth even though, so far, she'd only seen it looking unhappy.

Or maybe her reaction to him was because his mouth was pulled back into a frown.

This wasn't the time. She was letting her mind wander, taking her thoughts on a wild and very obviously purposeless chase.

She had to keep her mind on her goal. Getting out of here.

"Good," she declared.

Gayle began to look around the small enclosure for her clothes. And then another thought struck her. With a sense of foreboding, she had the uneasy feeling that she wasn't going to like the answer to her question.

Anticipating what he thought was Gayle's next move, Taylor bent down and removed the plastic shopping bag tucked just above the wheels of the gurney. When the nurse on duty had brought Gayle her one-size-fits-all hospital gown, she'd placed Gayle's bathing suit, as well as the shorts and tank top Jake had thought to bring with them, into the bag.

"Looking for these?" He held up the bag.

She took the bag from him mechanically, mumbling a thanks she was hardly aware of uttering. Gayle looked at Jake. There was only one way to find this out, and she might as well get it over with.

"Um, Jake, I can't remember." She caught her lower lip between her teeth and then forged ahead. "Where do I live?"

Taylor didn't wait for Jake to answer. "With me," he told Gayle. "You live with me."

She hadn't been prepared for the intense wave of panic that washed over her. It all but robbed her of her breath. "No, I don't," she insisted.

"Yes," Jake said to her, quietly but firmly, "you do."

Sam was right there to back him up. "He's right, you do."

She wanted to scream "No." To shout that the joke was over. But beneath it all was the strong, underlying fear that they weren't playing a trick on her. That for whatever reason, part of her memory was gone.

"Guys, you're scaring me."

"No more than you're scaring us," Taylor told her evenly.

She looked from one face to another, ending up with the man she wanted to believe was an impostor. Her eyes reverted back to Jake. Her throat suddenly felt dry, and her head began to spin again. She fought to keep from getting dizzy.

"Really?" she asked Jake, her voice hardly above

a whisper. She stared into her older brother's eyes, certain that if he was lying to her—the way she was fervently praying he was—she could tell. She could always tell when Jake was lying. He squinted.

"Really."

Jake wasn't squinting.

Shaken down to her very core, she sighed.

"Then why can't I remember?" she demanded, looking at Jake. Ever since she'd taken her first step, she'd fought to be independent, to be taken seriously on her own merit. But right at this moment, she wanted her big brother to take care of her. To make things right. "Why can't I remember anything about him?"

Jake ached for her as he struggled to make sense of all this. He took Gayle's hand in his. "We don't know, Gayle."

"The doctor said he doesn't even know," Sam chimed in, as if that could somehow make her feel better. That she wasn't the only one who didn't understand.

"Guys, could you leave us alone for a minute?" Taylor asked his brothers-in-law.

Panic returned, as raw and nearly as unmanageable as it had been that very first time her father made her jump into the water and swim on her own as he stood on the side of the pool. She'd flashed a confident smile, wanting to be his golden girl. But inside she'd been trembling. She'd been four at the time.

"No," Gayle cried, grabbing Jake's arm. She didn't want to be alone with this man. "Don't."

Very gently Jake peeled her fingers away from his forearm.

"We'll be right outside, Gayle," he promised, backing out of the area. A beat later Sam followed. Leaving the two of them alone.

For a moment Taylor stood there in silence. It was killing him, seeing her like this. Ever since he'd known her, Gayle had been vibrant, feisty. He couldn't ever recall her being frightened, the way she so visibly was now.

And then it came—that look he'd become so familiar with in the past year and a half. Defiance. Relief flooded over him, emotions threatening to close his throat. His Gayle was in there somewhere and he was going to go in and find her, even if he had to drag her out, kicking and screaming.

It would be like old times.

"Well?" she demanded, doing her best not to let this man see that she felt as if she was falling apart. She'd never been this frightened....

Except that she had, she suddenly realized. Something, just now, had flashed through her brain, a glimmer of a memory moving so fast she couldn't catch hold of it. All she could grasp was the hem of a fragment of fear. But fear of what or who, when and why, none of this had any answers.

Damn it, this was so frustrating. She felt like a book with all the even numbered pages missing.

Nothing made any sense to her. Least of all why she couldn't remember this man everyone told her was her husband.

"We'll take this slow, Gayle," Taylor promised. "One day at a time."

He fought the urge to take her into his arms and just hold her. Knowing that it was the last thing he should do. A hint of a smile formed as it occurred to him that if he did do that, she'd probably toss him across the room with one of those martial arts moves of hers. Martial arts had become her newest passion. Gayle did nothing by half measures. Whatever she undertook, she did so wholeheartedly.

It was the same when they made love.

God, he just had to bring her around. Had to make her remember their life together. And he didn't care what the doctor had said, he couldn't help but take this personally. She'd remembered everything. But him.

There had to be an underlying reason for that. The trouble was he wasn't sure he was going to like the answer once he found it.

She never took her eyes off him. He'd seen old tapes of Gayle at swim meets. She always watched her opponents the same way. Was that how she saw him? As an adversary?

"And meanwhile," she said, "I'm supposed to come home with you."

"It's where you live."

Gayle frowned. That's what *he* said, but how did

she know for sure? If she was his wife, wouldn't there be a degree of familiarity somewhere, however deep in her subconscious? If he was really her husband, the man she supposedly loved, would her mind really have shut down, excluding him from every thought, every memory?

She'd spent the past two hours sitting in a drafty hospital gown, waiting to be scanned and probed while she desperately tried to summon any kind of memories with him in them. All she'd managed to do was come up against a blank wall.

It had led her to an inevitable conclusion. If this man *was* her husband, then he must have been a terrible one. There was no other explanation why his very presence had been burned away from her memory banks.

Gayle drew herself up as high as she could manage. "I can stay with Sam or Jake." Her tone was deliberately dismissive. On a whim she added, "Just until I remember you." She thought that would put an end to any argument he might have.

Taylor shoved his hands into his pockets to keep from shaking her. A part of him still felt maybe this was payback for some imagined sin. She'd spent the first six months of their marriage testing him, as if she couldn't believe that he was going to stay and wanted him to go before she became used to her status. Used to him. He'd just dug in and waited her out. He didn't know if he had the stamina to do it again.

"The familiar surroundings might make you remember faster," he finally told her.

"Why should they be familiar if you're not?" she countered.

He threw up his hands, then struggled to regain control over his temper. Shouting at her wasn't going to accomplish anything. She *wasn't* testing him, he told himself. She was thrashing around in the same choppy waters that he was. It was up to him to lead her out of them. How, he had no idea, but he knew he was going to. There was too much at stake to just give up.

"I don't have any answers here, Gayle. The doctor doesn't have any answers," he emphasized. "This is all new territory for me."

She raised her hand as if she were sitting in a classroom, trying to catch the teacher's eye. "Let's not forget me here."

"I'm not forgetting you," he said so fiercely he knew he scared her. "Not for one damn second am I forgetting you. And I don't know why you seem to have forgotten me."

"Seem?" Gayle echoed, her temper flaring at the single word. She cleaved to the familiar feeling as if it was an old friend. This, this she could remember. Getting angry. Having no fear over voicing her opinions. She was her own person, no matter who this man was or wasn't to her. She had to remember that. "You think I'm faking this? That I'm pretending not to know you?"

For just a moment the bars he'd placed around his own temper seemed in danger of melting.

"Right now I don't know what to think," Taylor shot back. "You're not above doing things to bedevil me for reasons that I could never fully understand. You—"

Abruptly he stopped himself.

This wasn't the way to go, even though for him the ground was familiar. Arguing with Gayle might just push her farther into this black hole that had somehow eaten away at the part of her mind that had contained him.

Struggling for control, Taylor blew out a breath. He didn't need this. He pushed the plastic bag with her clothes closer to her. "Get dressed, Gayle. I'm going to take you home."

She clutched the bag against her, tossing her head the way he'd seen her do a hundred times before. Her long, blond hair flew over her shoulder. "No, you're not."

He leaned in close to her, his lips against her ear. "Yes," he said quietly, firmly, "I am."

His breath slipped along the curve of her neck. The shiver along her spine mimicked its path. Something in the distance stirred, although she could put neither name nor description to it.

She dropped it.

Although she didn't know him, something in the man's voice told her he wasn't someone to be messed with, to be disregarded. Certainly not a man she could order around the way she could so many of the others in her life. Even her brothers bent from time to time.

Just her luck, her so-called husband had a steel pole stuck up a place that should never be visited.

"I'll be back in a few minutes," he told her. With that Taylor pushed the curtain aside and walked out of her space.

He found Sam and Jake waiting for him in the hall where they'd talked to Peter.

Sam pretended to look him over carefully. "Well, no wounds," he observed. "That's a positive sign. Is Gayle coming around?" Taking a look at Taylor's face, Sam saw the answer to his question. Disappointment followed. "Guess not."

Taylor was struggling to take this newest development in stride, the way he had everything else that involved Gayle. "The woman's got the disposition of a wounded warthog."

Jake laughed. "Then she *is* coming around," he commented dryly. And then he looked at his brother-in-law. "Look, Tay, maybe Sam or I should take her in for a couple of weeks. I mean, if she doesn't remember you're married—"

Taylor cut him off. "She's going to remember, Jake. She'll see something, hear something, it'll trigger a memory and we can go from there. I've got to be there for that. Got to give her every opportunity to remember me. To remember us." He struggled to keep the hopelessness from absorbing him. "Maybe I'll show Gayle the wedding pictures."

"Might just do the trick," Sam agreed cheerfully, a strained smile pasted on his lips.

"You're a lousy actor, Sam," Taylor told him. "But thanks for trying."

He realized that Sam was no longer listening to him. Instead he was looking at something over his shoulder. Taylor turned around and saw that Gayle had emerged from out of the curtained area, wearing a white pair of impossibly short shorts and a white-and-pink-checkered blouse that tied above her midriff.

Her hair had long since dried and was hanging about her face and shoulders in tiny curls. She'd always told him that she hated the way that looked. He thought she looked beautiful.

Except for the hairstyle, she looked exactly the way she had when she'd stepped onto Sam's sloop this morning.

And yet she was different. She wasn't his Gayle anymore.

But she would be, he vowed. She would be.

"God, I look like Orphan Annie," she complained, spiking her fingers through her hair and trying to pull it straight. It was an exercise in futility.

"Orphan Annie she remembers," Taylor muttered under his breath.

But Gayle heard him. "Sure, I used to read the comic strip every day when I was a kid," she said as she moved closer to Jake and away from him.

Closer to what was familiar. Away from what was not.

Chapter Four

"Well, this place isn't going to win the *Good Housekeeping* award anytime soon."

Gayle stood in the doorway of the house her "husband" claimed to be theirs. A distant feeling of déjà vu whispered through her, but then in the next moment it was gone.

She didn't recognize the house, and she had a feeling she would have, given its unique state.

Gayle remained where she was, holding on to the doorknob. Not wanting to let go.

Not wanting to take a step farther into this house she didn't recognize, into this life she didn't know with a man who was a stranger to her.

Stalling, she looked around. A clear plastic tarp hung from the ceiling to the ground and furniture clustered together in the middle of the room like marooned survivors of a shipwreck. The furniture, a sofa, love seat, coffee table and two side tables were covered with more plastic tarp.

The wall to her left had holes in it, courtesy of the sledgehammer leaning against it. Sanders, saws and a variety of equipment she didn't readily recognize were scattered throughout the area she assumed had once been a living room. Here and there, hints of olive-green wallpaper still clung for dear life to the walls that remained intact.

It looked like the center of her worst nightmare. She *lived* here?

Taylor slowly pocketed his key. He couldn't close the door because she was still blocking the sill. His eyes never left her face as he waited and prayed for some ray of recognition to cross it. All he saw was startled wonder.

"We live here," she finally said, looking at him. It wasn't so much a question as a statement rimmed in disbelief.

"Yes." It was a work in progress and because of another job he'd taken on, progress had been slow and limited. The shoemaker's children went barefoot, he thought cryptically. "Why don't you come away from the doorway, Gayle?"

She gave no indication that she heard him. Instead Gayle looked up at the unfinished ceiling.

Squinting, she could see that it had been recently scraped and then textured. The surface seemed brighter than the rest of the room, even though it was obviously waiting for a final coat of paint.

Gayle's eyes shifted to his. "I'm afraid something might fall on me if I come in."

Taylor looked around, trying to see through her eyes. It wasn't easy. What he usually saw even when he looked at a place that was crumbling was potential. Always potential. He supposed that was where he channeled whatever optimism he possessed.

"Don't be. The house is rock solid. I thoroughly checked out the foundations before we signed the mortgage papers."

Mortgage papers. For some reason she'd just assumed they were renting the house. It was more in keeping with this temporary feeling that nibbled away at her.

She looked at him. Why in heaven's name would they have wanted to buy such a place? "We own this."

"Yes," he answered evenly. He knew her well enough to know that he should be bracing himself for the onslaught of something.

Gayle moved away from the doorway. Proximity did not improve on her impression. This was a disaster area. All it needed was to be declared so by the governor.

"Why?" she asked. "Did we lose a bet?" Gayle crossed to the ventilated wall. The gaping holes where sledgehammer had met plywood gave her a view of another room. The latter was decorated in colors and styles that had been popular roughly thirty years ago. She did her best to stifle a shiver and succeeded only marginally. "This place is falling apart."

"No," he corrected, following her as she conducted her inspection. "I'm taking it apart."

When she was growing up, her father had considered hammering a nail into the wall to hang a picture major construction. For anything else he always hired help, laborers. Physical labor was something to be avoided. "Why?"

He could remember Gayle taking an interest, not only in this house, but in the ones he worked on. Had she feigned that? Or was she now just trying to find the path back and, once there, her interest, her enthusiasm would return? "Because it's what I do for a living."

Gayle looked around again, then back at him. She'd always assumed that when she did get married, it would either be to a professional athlete or a professional *something,* like a doctor or a lawyer. But apparently she was supposed to have tied the knot with a laborer. "You destroy houses for a living?"

"Renovate," Taylor corrected evenly, "the word is *renovate.*"

He thought he saw her frown slightly. Before he could tell himself that it was his imagination, impatience bit into him. He'd been pushed to the edge today and wasn't sure just how much more he could take before he was on overload. He'd been half-terrified out of his mind when he thought that he'd lost Gayle, then relieved when he'd found her.

But now he was faced with the same situation, only in a different form. He *had* lost Gayle, at least temporarily. Because she couldn't remember him. Couldn't react to him the way only a wife could to the man she entrusted all her secret hopes and dreams to. A man who'd been privy to all the private moments that went into making Gayle who and what she was.

Or had been, he amended silently.

Frustrated, Taylor wanted to shout "Game over!" and have her the way she'd been just this morning, before they'd taken off for Jake's sloop.

Damn, he wished they'd never stepped foot on that stupid hunk of overpriced, floating ballast. More than anything in the world, he wanted her to look at him the way she did when it was just the two of them, and the world was fading away.

Instead it seemed as if he was the one who had apparently faded away for her.

"You don't remember this?" He asked the question even though he already knew what her answer would be.

Gayle turned on her heel to face him. "I don't remember *you*," she needlessly reminded him.

She pressed her lips together, trying desperately to keep the sharp edge of panic from growing into unmanageable proportions the way it had earlier.

She needed to keep moving. If this man looking

at her so intently really was who he said he was, well, he had to prove it to her, to make her remember him. He had all the cards. She had nothing to draw on. No special place to retreat to in order to start all over again, rebuilding memories.

She *had* no memories, at least none of him. He had to do something that would change that, not her.

It suddenly occurred to Gayle that she was lacking the most basic form of information. She tried to remember if one of her brothers had called out to her would-be husband and failed to come up with anything. "I don't even know your name."

"Taylor. Taylor Conway." He shoved his hands into his back pockets. This felt so stupid, introducing himself to his wife of eighteen months.

"And I'm Gayle Conway?" She rolled the name over on her tongue, testing it out. Tasting it. Listening to the way it sounded. No sense of the familiar came washing over her, yet she did recognize the name as belonging to her.

"Privately," he told her. "Professionally you're still Gayle Elliott. You work at—"

"KTOC, yes, I know." She had a very clear image of her small dressing room. Her section of the desk on the set, beneath glaring lights. She loved the life.

He felt as if a paring knife had slipped in beneath his third rib. And he had to wait awhile before this stopped bothering him so much. Maybe they'd get lucky and she'd regain her memory by then. "You remember your job."

"I like referring to it as a career."

There were times when she thought it was somehow unethical, being paid for doing something she loved so much. She would have paid the station to allow her to mingle with professional athletes, follow certain teams when they went on the road to play in other cities, reporting it all back to hungry viewers who weren't as lucky as she was.

He felt as if something was about to snap inside of him. What if she *never* remembered him? Never remembered the past eighteen months?

Taylor grasped her by the shoulders. "Damn it, Gayle, if you're putting me on—"

She watched him unflinchingly, the strength of his fingers registering as they pressed hard against her biceps. "Why would I put you on about that?"

Belatedly he realized he must be holding her too tightly, that he was channeling his frustration through his fingers.

Taylor dropped his hands to his sides. "You know what I mean." Taking a breath, he got himself under control again and muttered, "Sorry." It was the fear that had made him behave this way. Fear of losing what they'd had.

"That wasn't easy for you, was it?" When he gave her a slow, puzzled look, she said to clarify, "You don't like apologizing."

Hope sprang up like toast out of an overly eager toaster. "You remembered that?"

He'd looked so hopeful that she'd almost lied. But

this was about getting down to the truth, not lying. "Sorry, no. Instinct," she explained. "I'm pretty good at reading people."

He should have realized it wasn't going to be that easy. Still, he couldn't help being resentful. "So how come you erased me out of your book?"

She began to say "If I did," but the phrase never left her mouth. Saying that would only be adversarial. By now she knew there was no *if*. She apparently *had* erased Taylor. Her brothers wouldn't have deliberately allowed him to take her "home" to this half-destroyed bomb shelter if she really wasn't married to him.

"I don't know," she told him honestly. "I don't know." Blowing out a breath, Gayle took a whimsical stab at the reason behind the lapse. "Maybe you beat me."

Taylor stared at her. "What? No," he denied vehemently when the full impact of her words registered. "I didn't beat you. If I'd raised a hand to you, you would have been all over me like a Tasmanian devil." He realized that she could misinterpret that, as well. "Not that I ever would raise a hand." And then, because there had been so much between them, he added, "Although, a saint would have trouble living with you at times."

Her eyes grew into small slits. "And you're no saint."

There was an argument here, but he couldn't allow himself to be drawn into it. Couldn't banter with her for the sake of bantering. She no longer knew him and there was so much she could misunderstand. So he merely said, "No, I'm not."

Questions began to form in between the holes of her thoughts. "Did we get along?"

"Yes," he said with feeling, then qualified it. "Sometimes."

She jumped to the other side, as was her habit. "And sometimes not?"

He lifted a shoulder in a casual shrug. "Like I said, you had your moments."

"And you didn't?"

There were times when he rose to the bait. Or baited her. "Yeah, me, too."

It sounded as if they fought a lot. Which brought her to another conclusion and hopefully the answer she was looking for. "Were we getting a divorce?"

"No," he retorted adamantly. "Hell, no. What made you ask that?"

It was her turn to shrug. When she did so, the strap of her tank top slid off her right shoulder. "Trying to get to the bottom of why my brain pressed the delete button on you."

Any other time he might have pushed down the other strap, taking the material all the way down to her waist. But this wasn't the time to give in to the desires she always aroused within him. He had a feeling that making love with her right now wouldn't trigger anything except maybe a five-alarm scream.

So he trod lightly, hoping she'd return to her right

mind—and him—soon. "The doctor said there might not be a reason."

That wasn't very encouraging, she thought. Gayle moved away from the wall. It reminded her too much of what her brain felt like. "Then we're at less than square one."

He looked at her for a long moment. "I don't know about that. You're here."

That wasn't saying very much, she thought as she looked around. Although, she could have forced one of her brothers to take her in, she supposed. Why hadn't she? She wasn't really sure.

"In a war zone," she observed.

Because each project was a labor of love for him, especially this one, he took offense. "It's not as bad as all that."

"Yeah," she agreed, "we could be living outdoors and it could be the rainy season."

Okay, there was a glimmer of a grin there, he was sure of it. Some of her humor was surfacing. He took heart in that.

"You actually liked helping me," he told her. Placing his hand on her shoulder, Taylor brought her over to the largest gaping hole in the wall. "See that?"

She'd have to be blind not to, she thought. "What about it?"

"You did that," he told her. She looked at him in disbelief. "You called it therapeutic. Said it helped you get rid of your aggression. Want to try doing it now? You always had a lot to spare."

Was that criticism, she wondered. Or was he daring her? Never one to let a challenge go unanswered, she picked up the sledgehammer. The weight surprised her. "Heavy."

"You swung it like a pro. All that upper-body strength you developed as a swimmer," he explained, telling her what she had once told him when he'd marveled at the way she wielded the hammer.

Another woman would have claimed it was too heavy to use, but Gayle always saw things like that as a challenge. He'd never met anyone who loved being challenged as much as she did.

He was counting on that now, hoping she would view reconstructing the pieces of her life with him as a challenge.

Hefting the hammer, Gayle took one long, measured swing, making contact with the wall. A shower of plaster, ugly wallpaper and plywood went flying in all directions. A sense of exhilaration blasted through her.

"You're right," she declared, bracing to take another swing, "this does feel good."

But as she began to swing the sledgehammer, Taylor grabbed the hammer's wooden shank and stopped her.

She glanced at him defiantly, still holding the hammer with both hands. "What?"

"Maybe you shouldn't tire yourself out right now." His eyes skimmed over the bandage on her forehead. "You did get that head injury."

"Oh, that." Reluctantly Gayle relinquished the hammer. She slid her fingertips gingerly over the bandaged area and raised her eyes to his. "Think this was the part that remembered you?"

He had no idea how the mind worked or, even if he did, how hers worked. She had always been a mystery to him, but he had just begun finally learning. He didn't want to give all that progress up.

"I'd like to think I had more than a microchip-size hold on your life." He leaned the sledgehammer in the same spot against the wall, then looked at her. "Are you hungry?"

Gayle paused to think. Until now she hadn't thought in terms of food. She'd been too consumed trying to straighten out the tangled mess her life had suddenly become. But it looked as if there were no easy solutions. She hated that.

"I guess. Maybe just an apple."

At least that hadn't changed, he thought. Gayle had always liked to eat healthy. That was her father's influence. The choices were almost too healthy for his tastes.

But there were occasional pizza breakdowns, and he lived for that.

He decided to give it a shot now. "How about a pizza?" he suggested. "I can order in."

About to say no, Gayle changed her mind and shrugged. "Okay." Maybe if that was what they normally did, it might seem familiar enough to her to cause her to start to remember.

She watched as Taylor dialed a number he seemed to have committed to memory. Did they eat like this often? Did it annoy him that she couldn't cook?

The man was incredibly sexy and good-looking. *Why* was there no memory of him? Why had only he and this house vanished from her mind and nothing else?

Suddenly needing to test herself, Gayle began to pull random bits and pieces out of the air. Her social security number. The address of her father's house. The date she won her first swim meet. Each and every one of them returned to her with ease.

Why not him?

There *had* to be a reason. There just had to be.

It felt almost like a first date.

That same uneasy awkwardness shimmered between them. The awkwardness of two strangers exploring each other, trying to decide if this was a colossal mistake or the beginning of something really good.

Except that a lot was at stake here, Gayle reminded herself as she finished what had to be her final piece of pizza. Only two pieces were left in the box. Far smaller than Taylor, she had consumed as much food as he had.

In the background, a popular police drama was just wrapping up an episode on the TV. For the sake of spending the evening in so-called familiar surroundings, she had feigned interest in the program, although her interest had waned once she'd guessed the killer's identity and the reason behind his crime spree.

She wished she could come up just as easily with the reason behind her brain's vanishing act when it came to Taylor.

He picked up a napkin and wiped the grease from his fingers. "You're awfully quiet."

"Just thinking."

"Maybe you shouldn't."

Was this some kind of male suppression on his part? She certainly didn't have a handle on who he was yet. He seemed nice enough. But that wasn't enough for a marriage, was it? "I shouldn't think?"

"Shouldn't try so hard to remember," he clarified. "Let it come."

"You're awfully calm for a man whose wife doesn't remember him."

He smiled. At least she wasn't denying that any longer—that she was his wife. He took that as a sign of progress. "You should see my insides."

She glanced toward the screen. The program had been one of those that took pleasure in taking the viewer on a visual, internal tour of every organ the deceased possessed.

"No, thanks, I think I've seen enough insides for one night." She paused, chewing on a new thought.

He could swear he could see the wheels turning in her head. "What?"

She raised her eyes to his. "Were we…you know…happy?"

He'd expected a more-intimate question. Maybe it had been and she'd lost her nerve at the last moment. No, he decided, Gayle didn't lose her nerve. She charged headlong into any battle, any situation.

He looked at her for a long moment, trying to summon the woman he loved to the surface. And failing. "We had our moments."

That sounded rather sad and lonely. "Just moments?"

He laughed. "Sometimes longer than that. We fought," he admitted. "We made up." There was fondness in his voice as he recalled some of their more aggressive times. She made love like a wild woman, bringing out the full spectrum of passion from him. "That's what made it all worth it. The making up."

His eyes held hers. And then he reached for her.

The second he did, Gayle slid back as far as she could on the sofa. Her eyes were accusing. "What the hell do you think you're doing?"

Trying to get my wife back. "I just thought of a way to jog your memory."

The next moment Gayle popped up to her feet, a jack-in-the-box exploding out of its confining tin container. There was no mistaking the look in her eyes.

"I just bet you did. Well, you can just hold on to that thought, buster—and not me. Am I making myself clear?" There was just no way she intended to make love with a complete stranger, no matter who the hell he said he was supposed to be or how damn good-looking he was. That just wasn't her.

On his feet, as well, Taylor dragged a hand through his jet-black hair, reining in the temper that only Gayle knew how to ignite. This was going to take a lot more patience than he'd anticipated.

Trouble was, he wasn't all that sure if he was up to it.

Chapter Five

He knew the anger he felt was largely unreasonable. This was a medical matter and nothing personal.

But it was hard not to take it personally when his wife, the woman he'd loved and let into the most private parts of his world—places no one else had ever been admitted to—kept rejecting him. Kept looking at him as if he were a stranger.

He did the best he could. "I know logic was never exactly your long suit, Gayle, but we did have a physical relationship."

"That was when I knew who you were," she retorted, frustration heating her reaction.

More than anything she hated not being in control, and if she couldn't remember him when he had supposedly been such an integral part of her life, then she wasn't in control, not even of her own mind and thoughts.

Taylor seized her response, cutting her off before she said something to negate the point he was trying to drive home.

"Exactly. And I just thought that kissing me might help you remember."

The crack about logic not being her long suit still had her bristling. "Remember what? That you're sarcastic?"

"No," he snapped, "that you loved me."

The phrase materialized in her mind's eye like a giant billboard. *That you loved me.* Had she? Until this morning's mishap, had she loved this man? A lot or a little? God, but she wished she had a grasp on that, at least a slight toehold.

She pressed her lips together, trying to sort out her feelings, which kept insisting on running helter-skelter, here and there, eluding organization. She felt some of her annoyance fading. He wanted to kiss her. To try to jar her memory.

It might be worth a try. Besides, the man was as good-looking as they came. As long as he didn't try to take things any further than a kiss, it might even be fun. After all, she wasn't a nun.

Gayle raised and lowered her shoulders with studied carelessness. "I suppose that makes some kind of sense."

This she hadn't forgotten how to do, to counter every word, every move from him with one of her own. Life with her at times was like an endless tennis game. He had to be on his toes constantly, never quite knowing when the next lob would land the ball.

"It makes perfect sense."

Gayle gave him a lofty look. "Nothing is perfect," she countered.

His eyes narrowed. *Was* she playing some kind of game? He just didn't know. "Living with you these past eighteen months made that pretty clear."

That stung. "If you're going to kiss me, then get it over with."

His temper made another reappearance. She made it sound like some kind of odious test she was forced to endure, he thought. "This isn't exactly in the same category as a root canal."

"How would I know that?"

Taylor knew he could answer her, could make some kind of retort to her challenge, but all that was going to be just a waste of breath and time. She'd just say something else and they'd go on thrusting and parrying indefinitely. Besides, if they continued this way much longer, the tender feelings he was hoping would come through wouldn't be there. She had a knack of making him reach his flashpoint in an incredibly short amount of time.

Struggling not to strangle her wasn't exactly the right frame of mind he needed in order to kiss her in a way that jarred the very foundations of her world. Or, at the very least, swept away the cobwebs from that part of her brain that seemed to have receded.

So instead of saying another word to her, Taylor hooked his arm around Gayle's waist, pulled her to him and, cupping the back of her head, brought his mouth down on hers.

Caught by surprise, she squirmed a little, wedging her hands against his chest. Had she pushed with any kind of strength or perceptible feeling, he would have immediately released her.

But she didn't.

As he put his heart and soul into the kiss, deepening it, Taylor became vaguely aware of Gayle's hands sliding almost bonelessly down the length of his pectorals. The very next second she was cleaving to him, her hands going around his neck as his blood was starting to rush in his veins.

This, he thought, this was his Gayle.

Maybe her mind didn't remember him, but it seemed as if her body did. It fit against him in that old, familiar way, her curves filling his spaces the way his filled hers. He remembered thinking, the first time they made love, that they were like two halves of a whole and that she made him feel complete.

He couldn't lose that, Taylor thought with an urgency that unsettled him.

The heat of her body penetrated his.

How could she respond like this and not remember him? his mind demanded just before all coherent thought faded into oblivion.

Wow. Oh, wow, Gayle thought. How could she not remember this man? He was both frying her hair and curling her toes at the same time. And she didn't even want to speculate about the condition her blood was in as it raced through her body, setting everything it came in contact with on fire.

Her head spun almost out of control, almost out of reach.

This was good. This was better than good; it was fantastic.

She couldn't catch her breath, didn't want to catch her breath, afraid that if she did, this wild ride she suddenly found herself on would stop.

Gayle was only marginally aware of pressing her body against his, although she was more than a little aware of the fact that her body seemed to have caught on fire in over a hundred different places.

She should remember this. *Why* didn't she remember this?

The question beat in her brain over and over again with the ferocity of a storm, even as she struggled to keep the moment from coming to an end. Her whole body felt as if it had been reduced to rainwater that had been left out in the sun and was now just about to sizzle away.

Moaning, she tightened her arms around his neck, pressing her lips harder against his.

Okay, Taylor thought, she remembered. She *had* to remember. She couldn't have kissed him this way with such feeling if she didn't.

God, but she'd had him scared there for a while.

His lips still sealed against hers, Taylor shifted and tucked one hand beneath her legs. Before he could begin to lift her off the floor, Gayle pulled her head back. Her hands were wedged against his chest again, pushing for all she was worth. The accident had done nothing to reduce her strength.

"What the hell do you think you're doing?" she demanded. Although fueled by anger, the question came out in short, staccato phrases because there was absolutely no air to spare in her lungs.

He stared at her, feeling like a man about to lose his mind. "I was going to take you to our bedroom."

"Put me down!" she ordered, sounding just like her father during a military drill. "Let me go!"

Disgusted, bewildered and not knowing just how much more of this emotional tennis game he was able to take, Taylor unceremoniously released her.

Survival instincts that were second nature to her ever since she'd first opened her eyes had Gayle grabbing his shoulders. The quick move was all that prevented her from crashing to the floor.

Straightening, she glared at him.

He returned the glare with an innocent look. "Just doing what you told me. Letting you go."

Gayle pressed her lips together, struggling to hold

on to a temper she knew could be explosive. The euphoria that he'd created just a few seconds ago had completely vanished.

"I also said just a kiss," she reminded him hotly. "That wasn't an invitation to drag me off to your lair, caveman style."

Taylor spread his hands out on either side of him, his fingers extended toward the ceiling in silent surrender. "Don't worry, I'm not about to take you anywhere near my 'lair.'"

But even as he said it, he realized that this was going to be their next immediate problem.

She saw the look on his face, knew he had just thought of something. "What?"

The master bedroom was the only room in the house that he had actually completed. Doing it had been a gift from him to Gayle for her birthday. The other three bedrooms, like the other rooms in the house, were all in varying stages of being gutted. Tools, tarps and piles of fallen plaster marked his progress or lack of it.

Taylor blew out a breath as he looked at her. "I suppose you want to take the master bedroom."

Ordinarily she wouldn't have hesitated, but she wasn't about to commit herself to anything inside this fun house. "That depends."

He had no idea where she was going with this. "On what?"

"On whether or not it looks as if the unibomber tried testing out some of his creations in it before moving on. Does it have walls?" she asked.

Given the state of the living room, he supposed it was a legitimate question. It had been too much to hope for that she remembered all the work he had put into it for her. "Yes, it has walls."

She wasn't satisfied. "A door?"

He bit back his impatience. "Why don't you come and see for yourself?" Taylor motioned for her to follow him as he led the way to the stairs. He'd taken off the original banister and replaced it with one made out of finely sanded alder wood. It needed to be painted. He deliberately refrained from touching it. Just as he was about to go up the steps, he abruptly turned around to look at her. "Back there, in the living room, when I kissed you—"

She had a feeling she knew what he was going to ask. What all men wanted to be told. How good they were. "It was nice," she grudgingly admitted.

This time he saw right through her. When she tried to avoid saying something, she wouldn't look at his eyes. "It was more than nice," he countered. "You felt something."

Her chin shot up. "Yes, I felt something. You, trying to get me into bed."

"Besides that."

He knew he was laying himself bare before the "old" Gayle, the woman his wife had been before they'd made that stunning connection that had rocked both their worlds, especially his. But he was trying to reach the woman she'd evolved into, the woman with whom the lovemaking threatened to burn right through any surface they were on. The woman he had exchanged vows and hearts with in the middle of a hospital chapel.

She wasn't that woman right now, not to him. But she had been. And if they were going to make any progress in that direction, one of them had to take the first step. It was obvious to him that Gayle wouldn't be the one. Though she tried to hide it, she was having enough trouble dealing with the scary knowledge that part of her wasn't the way it should be.

Even so, he felt like a man crossing Niagara Falls, inching his way along a tightrope made of dental floss. And there was no net in sight. "We connected just then."

With a shrug, she looked away, doing her best to sound indifferent. "If you say so."

Taylor took hold of her shoulders, forcing his wife to look at him, even as she tried to shrug him off. "Gayle, you're a hell of a lot of things, some good, some not so good, but you were never a liar."

She hadn't counted on his sensing her reaction. She should have disguised it better, she thought, up-braiding herself. No man was ever going to have control over her unless she wanted him to, and then only for a short, specified duration of her choosing.

"Okay," she conceded, annoyed, "we connected. If I was wearing socks, you would have knocked them off. But that doesn't change the fact that—"

"You still don't remember me," he concluded for

her. It was no longer an accusation, just a fact, one he swore he was going to change.

Gayle shook her head and, in his estimation, looked almost sad for a second. "I still don't remember you," she repeated.

Just for a moment it felt as if they were on the same team. "Maybe visual aids would help."

He saw her stiffen as she looked at him warily. "You're not going to take off your clothes, are you?"

He didn't know whether to laugh or take offense. Damn, but he wished he could peek into her head, figure out what she was thinking. But then, he'd never had a clear handle on that. He'd only gotten better at second-guessing her. Sometimes.

"I was thinking of wedding pictures."

"Oh." Wedding pictures. That sounded harmless enough. He had her worried for a minute. There was just something about him that made her feel he was an unquantified element, an unknown in the equation of her life. "All right." She looked around the chaos that he envisioned as a living room. "Where are they?"

"You keep them in our bedroom."

"*My* bedroom," she reminded him. "They're not lewd, are they?"

"They're wedding pictures," he emphasized. What did she think he was going to do, spring some kind of semipornographic photographs on her and try to pass them off as their wedding? "With your brothers and your father. You remember your father, right?"

Colonel Lars Elliott's voice was probably the first voice she could recall hearing.

Swim, Gayle, swim. You were born for the water. Make the colonel proud of you.

She'd always wanted to ask her father why he referred to himself in the third person every time he wanted his children to carry out an instruction. An edict was really more like it, she corrected herself. She could remember him running along the edge of the pool, barking out orders as she swam furiously from one end to the other. Always too slowly to please him no matter what her time turned out to be.

She could remember hating him at times for that. And trying harder the next time.

Gayle gave Taylor an impatient look. "Of course I remember my father."

"Of course," he echoed. Everybody and everything. Except for him.

A wave of contrition swept over her. She banked it down. Her tone was flippant in order to hide the spasm of guilt she didn't want to deal with. "Did I just hurt your feelings?"

Taylor stopped a few steps shy of their bedroom. The look he gave her was cold. "If I was capable of any sensitive feelings, marriage to you rubbed the sensitivity right out of me."

Another insult. Any guilt she felt vanished instantly. Squaring her shoulders, Gayle sailed right past him and into the bedroom.

It wasn't what she expected.

It wasn't a bedroom, it was a suite. A beautiful suite.

The extralarge room had a vaulted ceiling. On the far end was a small conversation pit, complete with a white flagstone fireplace. But what had caught her eye immediately was the huge, California king-size bed with its hand-quilted blue-and-white comforter, matching shams and a handful of throw pillows. The four-poster had lace curtains drifting down from a canopy frame. Power and femininity at the same time.

It was, quite literally, the bedroom of her dreams. Growing up, she'd been accustomed to almost Spartan conditions. Her father firmly believed that too many possessions spoiled a person, too much clutter led to an undisciplined mind and he didn't want any of his children to be either spoiled or undisciplined. And certainly not soft. He'd become a widower shortly after she was born and had approached the task of parenting the way he did everything else, militarily. She'd often said that the colonel hadn't tried to raise children so much as he'd raised short soldiers.

Life under her father's roof—and during his time in the military there had been many roofs—had been one major battle after another. Although there was no question that she loved the man dearly and wanted nothing more than to please him, they had butted heads almost from the moment she'd taken her first breath. Certainly from the moment she'd taken her first step. According to Jake, the colonel had wanted her to come to him, but instead she had made a wobbly path to the neatly arranged toy box. The lines were drawn then. She was too much like her father for the battles not to continue.

Gayle looked around slowly. The walls were painted a cool light blue, with white molding and white trim along the top and bottom.

"It's beautiful," she told him, her voice hardly above a whisper. "*You* did this?"

"I wanted to give you the bedroom of your dreams."

One night, she'd shared that with him, what she'd fantasized about while growing up. She'd wanted something soft, something pretty, yet something that still had an underlying strength to it. She'd confided the times that she felt trapped between two worlds, never living completely in either.

He'd given her words a visual interpretation, sketching the room he envisioned as soon as he could. Creating it became his number-one priority the moment they'd bought this house.

The look on her face the first time she'd seen the remodeled room had made all the hard work worth it.

The look resembled what was on her face now. Except then her next move had been to throw her arms around his neck with a joyous whoop, declaring that they needed to christen the bed as soon as possible.

They had, and even amid their rigorous love life, it had stood out as a night to remember.

She'd forgotten that, too, he thought with a sharp pang.

Crossing to the bed, Gayle picked up one of the curtains, examining it. The material felt soft, cool against her fingertips. She looked up at him. "You did this for me?"

He shrugged, burying his hands deep in his jeans. "Men don't usually go in for frills."

The look in his eyes got to her almost as much as his kiss had. He was making her weaken, she suddenly realized. With a little bit of encouragement…

She needed to push him away somehow. Now. She couldn't let herself be led around; she needed time, time to work this through for herself. To discover why it was she'd forgotten him when he'd apparently been so nice to her, at least some of the time,

She dropped the curtain and moved away from the bed, pretending to look out the window. A row of tall trees blocked her view of anything beyond the boundaries of the property.

"I guess that's kind of fortunate, then."

He didn't understand, but he braced himself. "What do you mean?"

Turning away from the window, she looked up into his eyes. "Because it looks like the rest of the rooms in this place definitely don't come with frills."

She was telling him to get out. "Right." He

crossed to the doorway. "Okay, if you need anything, I'll be right down the hall."

He hadn't made up his mind just which room to take. They were all pretty bad at this point, but in any event, all she needed to do was call out and he would hear her from whichever room he was in.

"I won't need anything," she assured him crisply.

Damn it. Gayle sounded like herself. She certainly kissed like herself. So why the hell wasn't she herself? And how long was this going to take? If he just had some finite point, some final date to reach and know that this ordeal was over, he could wait this out. The fact that the wait could be endless scared the hell out of him.

He crossed the threshold into the hall, then paused. "About tomorrow—"

Instantly she was on her guard. "What about tomorrow?"

"It's Monday," he told her. She went to the studio Monday through Friday when she wasn't on the road. "You have work."

What was he getting at? "Yes?"

She was making him feel like some kind of backward idiot. "I can call in for you," he said crisply, "tell them you're taking a few days off."

She was looking at him as if he was talking gibberish. "Why would I want to do that?"

"I don't know," he said in exasperation, "maybe to work at fixing this part of you."

"I'm not broken."

Taylor narrowed his eyes. "That might be a matter of opinion. You don't remember me," he reminded her, grinding out each word before pushing it through his clenched teeth.

"Maybe I have good reason," she retorted. "Did you ever stop to think about that?" He gazed at her for a long moment, then turned on his heel without saying another word. "Where are you going?"

"To get an aspirin. You've given me a headache. Again."

The word hung in the air long after he walked out of the room.

Again.

It didn't sound as if they had the best of marriages, she thought. Maybe that was what she was trying not to remember.

With a sigh, she crossed to the door and locked it.

Chapter Six

Taylor didn't hear him approach until Sam was nearly on top of him. Between the sawing and the hammering, the noise level was so intense inside the house he was currently renovating, he wore a pair of earphones to help block out some of it.

But even so, he might have been aware of Sam's presence if he hadn't been so lost in thought. He'd never been overly optimistic when it came to life. He liked to think he was prepared for some low blows, but no scenario he could have divined would ever have prepared him for Gayle suddenly not recognizing him, not being aware of his place in her life.

It just boggled his mind.

Gripping the handle of the sledgehammer tighter, he made contact with the concrete. The impact jarred him, traveling up the length of his arms through his biceps and triceps.

He swung again and again. Breaking up the concrete. Doing nothing to alleviate the dilemma in his soul.

The tap on his shoulder made him jump. Startled, Taylor just barely checked his swing as he turned around. Reality and the world returned. Sam was less than a foot away and had moved back quickly to avoid the unexpected contact.

"Damn it, Sam," Taylor growled, pushing his earphones off his head and down around his neck, "you came pretty damn close to having a hole where your stomach currently sits."

"Being a fireman makes you quick on your feet." Sam eyed the sledgehammer in his brother-in-law's hands. "You're swinging that hammer awfully hard, Tay." He took a calculated guess. "Working off steam?"

Rather than answer immediately, Taylor hefted the sledgehammer and took another hard swing at the wall. He'd been working on the Andersen place for the last month, devoting all his spare time to it. Unlike some of the other projects he'd undertaken, the people who owned this house still resided in their previous home. He could come and go as he pleased without worrying about having to accommodate the hours of a live-in family.

They'd given him six months to complete the job. This was month number two. His method was to gut all the rooms before he began transforming them. Usually he had a few day laborers to help, but this morning, except for Carlos whose only job was to cart away the debris, he'd decided to go at it solo.

"Something like that." He swung hard again. His arms began to feel rubbery. That meant he was going to have to take a break soon. "What are you doing here?" The hammer made contact with the wall again. "Don't you have some fire to put out or a Dalmatian to wash?"

Sam stood off to the side, for the most part avoiding the dust coming from the fallout. "It's my two days off and the Dalmatian and I have an agreement. I don't wash him, he doesn't lick me."

Exhaling, Taylor decided to take a break and put the sledgehammer down, its head resting on the floor while its handle pointed straight up. "You just had a couple of days off. What about this Sunday?" That was why they'd all gone on Jake's sloop. It was one of the rare times that all four of them could coordinate their schedules so that they could get together.

Sam smiled fondly at his brother-in-law. Technically, Taylor was right. Concern had him down here today, just as it had taken him to first look in on Gayle. He'd caught her just as she was hurrying off to the studio. For a woman who had nearly drowned and was now walking around without any memory of her husband, Gayle seemed in amazing health and spirits. But then, his sister had always been able to mask what was going on inside of her. He'd let it go for the time being, promising himself to look in on her later.

"I just put in for some personal time," Sam said dismissively, "but I'm not down here to talk about my work schedule."

"Why are you down here?" Taylor checked his growl at the last moment. He was still trying to get used to this all-for-one-and-one-for-all mentality that governed his wife and her brothers' approach to life. He'd grown up keeping to himself and the transition wasn't easy. But he was working on it.

"To find out how things went last night." Sam's mouth curved again. "I guess that growl kind of answers my question. Gayle still doesn't remember being married to you, huh?"

"Or so she says," Taylor said.

He saw the wary look on Sam's face, as if his brother-in-law was torn between whose side to take. Thirsty, he went over to his cooler and took out a bottle of water. He offered another to Sam, who passed.

Unscrewing the top, Taylor took a long drag from the plastic bottle before continuing. "I'm still not a hundred percent convinced this isn't some trick she's playing." Especially after she'd kissed him back.

Sam shook his head. "I really don't think she'd carry on a joke like that for more than a few hours, Taylor."

Granted, she hadn't up until now, but that didn't mean she couldn't. "What makes you so sure?"

"Well, for one thing, she loves you. For another, she gets bored easily."

"Maybe it's not a joke, maybe it's payback of some kind."

Sam stared at him. "Payback? For what?"

Taylor drained the rest of the water, then tossed the bottle into a special container separate from the rest of the garbage. That was Gayle's doing. She'd made him promise to put recyclables in a special pile. Everywhere he turned, she'd left an imprint, an indelible mark on his life to show that she'd passed through. Why hadn't he left an indelible mark on hers?

"Who knows? With Gayle, it could be anything. There was that time she thought one female client of mine was coming on to me." He still remembered that jealous expression on her face, how it had made her seem even sexier. "I slept on the couch for a week until I convinced her there was nothing going on, that even if the woman was standing there, stark naked, I wouldn't care because I loved only her." They'd had the best makeup sex that night, he recalled.

Damn it, he wanted his wife back.

"Making you sleep on the couch sounds like Gayle," Sam agreed, following him back to the half-demolished family room wall. "The amnesia bit doesn't."

Reluctantly Taylor nodded. "Maybe you're right." Facing that frightened him most of all. A prank he knew how to handle, was good at retaliating. But how did he deal with a mind that had suddenly shut him out in earnest? What did he do to get through to her again?

At a loss, he dragged his hand through his hair. "But if you are, then I'm really up the creek, Sam. How do I make her remember me?"

"The wedding album didn't work?"

"She recognized all of you, but not the event. And not me. Not from that day, anyway." Frustrated, he scrubbed his hands over his face. "I'm just the guy hovering at her elbow, claiming to be her husband." It wasn't easy admitting that, but he was as close to Sam and Jake as he was to anyone.

Except for Gayle. But it wasn't as if she was exactly available to him at the moment.

Taylor gave voice to the biggest fear that haunted him. "What if she never remembers me?"

Although he was a fireman, Sam never dealt in worst-case scenarios. He always looked on the positive side of everything, even if the light had been temporarily turned off.

"Not going to happen," he assured Taylor. "Look, until you came along, Jake and I thought she'd never get married. That no one could get into the ring and last even three minutes with her. You not only lasted the three minutes, you lasted the whole damn championship match." He grinned at the man he'd come to regard with affection as another brother. "All fifteen rounds. We never saw her like that with anyone else, and believe me, there were a lot of guys who came around. Most of them, she didn't even pay any attention to. *You're* the one who melted down her resistance. Because you hung in there."

The words in the last sentence were uttered slowly, each word a little slower than the one that came before it as he tried to reinforce his sentiment.

Taylor looked at him. "Okay, Sam, what are you thinking? I can almost see the smoke coming out of the top of your head."

Sam's grin went from one ear to the other. "Court her."

Taylor looked at his brother-in-law as if he'd lost his mind. "What?"

"Court her," Sam repeated. "Do whatever it was you did the first time around. It worked once, who's to say it won't work again?"

"Court her?" Taylor echoed incredulous. Men didn't court their wives. Jumping through those kinds of hoops was for before the vows. There was a whole different set to jump through after the wedding took place. "That's ridiculous, Sam. She's my wife, not my girlfriend."

"But she doesn't remember being either," Sam pointed out. "Besides, there's nothing wrong with courting your wife."

Spoken like a man who'd never been married, Taylor thought darkly. Besides, he didn't have time to go through what he had initially. He had a house to finish.

But then he thought of how he'd felt, spending the night on the floor of one of the other bedrooms last night. They'd spent time apart before, when she was on the road. But he'd always known when she was coming back to him.

He didn't know that anymore.

Taylor frowned. Gayle would never go for it. She was far too suspicious. "There is when she acts like you're some sexual predator."

"You lost me." And then, just as quickly, the light dawned on Sam. "You didn't try to get her into bed, did you?"

"I kissed her," Taylor snapped. Getting her into bed had been a goal—for purely altruistic reasons, he told himself. Intimacy might have triggered something in her head. "Not that it's any business of yours."

"She's my sister and part of her brain cells have gone missing, so, yes, for the time being it is my business," Sam countered evenly. "Once she's okay, you guys can act out all the parts of Hamlet stark naked for all I care."

"There's a thought," Taylor muttered, shaking his head.

It occurred to Sam that both his sister and Taylor were bullheaded and stubborn. "Here's another one. Did you two have some kind of a major fight before you came to the sloop on Saturday?"

Taylor shook his head. "No, nothing out of the ordinary." He thought back beyond Saturday. "Maybe she's been a little moody lately, but I just chalked that up to jet lag. The station sent her out on assignment five times last month. She was looking a little pale. That's why I thought going out on the boat would be a good idea."

"So there's no reason why she'd try to forget you."

"Of course not," Taylor said, doing his best to suppress his anger.

Sam spread his hands. He was out of ideas. "Back to courting her."

Taylor blew out a long breath, resisting the notion. "It's a dumb idea."

Sam plucked a plastic bottle out of the cooler and took off the cap. He cocked his head, looking at Taylor before he took a swig. "Got a better one?"

Taylor hated to admit it, but right now, he was stumped. "No."

Sam took only a sip before saying, "Then give it a try until something else comes up. You won her once, you can do it again."

"I don't have to 'win' her, I have her," Taylor protested, but there was a lack of feeling behind his words. If he had her, she wouldn't have shut him out of their bedroom.

Sam gave him a long, searching look. "Do you?" Before Taylor could say anything in protest, Sam glanced at his watch. "Look, I've got to run. I told Cynthia I'd help paint her bedroom."

Sam had a very healthy love life. Taylor wasn't sure, but he thought this was a new name. He wasn't exactly thinking clearly this morning. "Cynthia?"

A brilliant smile lit up Sam's boyish face. "This really hot little dental assistant I saved when her sister's place caught on fire. Cynthia was house-sitting for her at the time."

And not doing the best job, Taylor thought. But then, Sam didn't go in for the brainy type. He liked them long-legged, curvy and blond. Being a nuclear physicist was never a requirement. "Sounds like you got yourself a winner, there."

"The fire wasn't her fault," Sam replied already making his way toward where the brand-new double doors had been put in. "And think about what I said."

"Yeah yeah, I'll think about it," Taylor said, picking up his sledgehammer again. Braced, he turned his attention to the wall. He began swinging even harder this time.

"You do that, Tay," Sam murmured under his breath as he closed the door behind him.

Gayle waited until she heard the car pull out of the driveway and she was sure that Taylor had left the house. The moment she was, she hurried back upstairs to the bedroom she didn't remember beyond last night. After closing the door, she then crossed to the richly carved armoire and opened the bottom drawer. There, right on the top was the wedding album Taylor had shown her the night before.

Holding her breath, she took it out. She wanted to look at the photographs again, this time without having him hover over her. Gayle carried it over to the four-poster bed and sat down. Very carefully, she examined it page after page, as if she was hunting for a clue to an unsolvable mystery.

The album was at least five inches thick, and every page had at least one photograph of her with her so-called husband. Holding hands, kissing, laughing. It looked as if she'd had a wonderful time at the wedding, as if she was very happy.

Gayle sighed. The day a woman got married was supposed to be one of the happiest days of her life. So why couldn't she remember that day?

Why couldn't she remember him?

"What happened between us, Taylor?" she whispered to the man in photograph. It was of the two of them, kissing in front of the wedding cake. "What did you do to make me forget you?"

Maybe it wasn't his fault, she thought. Maybe she had done something, and the guilt she'd felt had leaped into action at the accident, causing her to wipe him out of her memory banks.

Her heart began to hammer. Gayle snapped the album shut on her lap. Could that be it? Could she have done something, maybe been unfaithful to Taylor in a moment of weakness and her mind couldn't deal with that so she'd just shut down that part of her brain that kept everything about him, about them, stored away?

"That's ridiculous," she declared heatedly to the silence around her.

Maybe she couldn't remember him, but she remembered herself, and she knew she'd never do something like that. Getting off the bed, she went to the armoire and put the album back in the bottom drawer. To the best of her recollection, she'd never been a party girl. She dated a lot, but sleeping with men took an emotional commitment she wasn't willing to volunteer.

She enjoyed being with men, enjoyed their company. Enjoyed flirting with them, she always had. As long as it remained on a harmless level. Everyone knew that she didn't hop into bed as a way of ending an evening of partying. So there was no reason to believe that she would have violated her marriage vows on a whim.

Marriage vows she didn't remember taking, she thought, holding her head.

It was beginning to ache again, just as it did yesterday in the E.R. Normally she tried to tough it out through any pain, but she didn't feel up to it right now. Not this early in the day. She had a segment to tape at the studio.

With a sigh Gayle went into the master bathroom to take one of the painkillers the E.R. doctor had prescribed. Unlike the rest of the house, it, too, was finished. Done in cool blues and white. Like the bedroom, the bath area was huge.

She could have held a party right here, she mused,

opening the mirrored cabinet. There certainly was enough room.

The thought whispered along her brain, as if trying to coax something forth. *Had* she hosted a party here? A party for two, maybe? With Taylor?

But as she concentrated, even the wisps of a distant memory disappeared.

Swallowing the tablets, she closed the cabinet again. If she didn't hurry, she was going to wind up late to the studio. And she was *never* late. That was something her father had ingrained in her.

"Why didn't you tell me?"

The makeup girl had just vacated the small, neat dressing room where, Monday through Friday, she got ready for in-studio broadcasts. By her watch, Gayle had fifteen minutes before she was to tape part of the loop that was to be shown for the rest of the day as well as the evening and night broadcast. It would feature her recounting of yesterday's sports highlights. Now, at the tail end of summer, the baseball play-offs were getting closer and closer and the Angels were still battling for the number-one spot in the American League's western division. Her Friday interview with Damien Miller, by all accounts, hottest new pitcher in the league was going to be used in the loop before she segued into the baseball scores.

She'd just been going over all the main points she had to get in for the three-minute segment when her door opened again. Flew open, actually. And this time there'd been no knock.

"Why didn't you tell me?" The repeated question echoed in the clutter-free dressing room.

Tall, muscular, with silver-gray hair and an air of unshakable strength about him, the man strode into the dressing room as if he owned it. Like the kings he claimed were in his ancestry, Colonel Lars Elliott seemed to own every piece of ground he crossed. It remained his until he chose to relinquish it.

"Hello, Colonel," Gayle said mildly, putting down her notes. The look she gave him was studied innocence. "Tell you what?"

His dark eyebrows came together like two iron-gray tufts. "That you almost drowned."

"But I didn't," she said cheerfully. "Otherwise, you'd be bursting into someone else's dressing room."

His look only grew darker. "Don't get flippant with me."

Her smile remained in place. She found that usually undermined some of his frontal attacks. "Just pointing out the obvious."

The colonel snorted. The look on his face had been known to weaken the knees of a good many brave men. "The obvious is that you don't seem to have a brain in your head."

He'd stopped scaring her somewhere around the age of five. That was the first time she'd stood up to him. The battle had gone on ever since.

"Oh, but I do," she told him brightly. "The technicians at Blair Memorial Hospital took quite a few scans of it and according to them there was something there every time."

"What are you doing here?" He waved one powerful hand around the dressing room. "You should be home resting," he told her, his face close to hers.

She struggled to keep her expression cheerful. "I'm fine."

His temper was in danger of igniting. "Then why don't you remember your husband?"

She gave up the charade as a hint of her own temper surfaced. "Who talked to you? And why aren't you in Nevada, visiting Aunt Nell?"

"I'm here because Jake called to tell me about your accident."

There were times when her big brother was just too damn responsible. "Good old Jake, looks like I owe him one."

"At least Jake has some sense in his head." As the colonel drew himself up, the room somehow became smaller. "You're coming home with me." His tone said he would brook no nonsense from her.

He took her by the arm but Gayle pulled her hand back. She wasn't about to be ordered around like some five-year-old. She had resisted then and she certainly wasn't going to go along with it now. "Why would I be coming home with you?"

The colonel struggled to hold on to the edge of his temper. Gayle had been a trial since the day she was born. "Because your so-called husband obviously doesn't think enough of you to take care of you."

A shimmer of protectiveness toward Taylor rose within her. She could only attribute it to the fact that there were times when her father said "black" that made her want to shout "white." It had nothing to do with Taylor.

"No one takes care of me but me, Colonel. Now the E.R. doctor checked me out from head to toe. I put up with a lot of pricy scans to prove it. He signed me out, saying I was fine."

"If you're so 'fine,'" her father countered, "why can't you remember Taylor?"

"The doctor said that when a blow to the head is involved, sometimes people get amnesia."

"Amnesia, maybe, but they don't just forget one person. Not unless something terrible happened. I've seen it with soldiers." He was talking about post-traumatic stress disorder, she thought. That wasn't what was responsible for the gaping hole in her memory, was it? "Now I won't pry and ask what the trouble is between the two of you," her father was saying, "but until it's resolved, you can stay in your old room."

She knew he was only trying to be kind in his own fashion, but she wasn't about to slip under his thumb this way.

"Thank you, but no. I'm working this out on my own, Colonel. Now, thank you for worrying about me, but please go back and finish your visit with Aunt Nell. I'll be fine," she insisted. "I *am* fine."

He glared at her. "Never could talk any sense into that fool head of yours. If you were a soldier, I would have had you thrown into the brig."

She smiled up at him brightly again. "Then I guess I'm lucky I'm not a soldier." And then she grinned in earnest. "If I'm stubborn, you have no one else but yourself to blame, Colonel. Everyone says I take after you."

His expression was impassive as he looked at her. "I knew my place."

"No, you didn't," she countered, her grin never fading. "Aunt Nell told me stories."

"The old blabbermouth." And then his expression softened. "You'll call me if you need me?"

She pointed to her cell phone on the vanity table. "Got you on my speed dial."

"That doesn't answer my question."

There was a knock on her door. "Two minutes, Gayle."

"That's my cue," she told her father, getting up. "I've got to go."

The colonel took hold of her by her shoulders and looked at her for a long moment. Then he released her without saying a word. She knew that, while she drove him crazy because they clashed so often, her father was proud of the fact that she never visibly buckled.

Even when she would have secretly wanted to.

Keeping her smile in place, Gayle left the dressing room.

Chapter Seven

Taylor stopped dead the moment he closed the door behind him. Almost immediately he came up against what appeared to be yellow tape, run amok.

Gayle was on the far side of the living room. Her head had jerked up the second he'd walked in. Their eyes met as he demanded, "What the hell is this?"

He'd been purposely late getting home, secretly hoping that once he walked through the doorway, he'd find that things had gone back to normal.

Or as normal as they could be, given that he was married to a woman who insisted on making everything around her a challenge of some sort. She brought excitement into the word hello and while at times he found keeping up with her exhausting, the life he was living now was a considerable improvement over the existence he'd had before he met Gayle.

Funny thing was, he hadn't realized just how lackluster his life had been until he had something to compare it to. Like the difference between living in the recesses of a cave and camping out in the sunlight.

Gayle, God help him, was his sunlight.

Except that, with one look at her face he knew that his sun was in danger of going nova.

It didn't help matters to discover yellow tape running through the length of the newly gutted living room.

Gayle took a few steps toward him. "Oh, you're home."

She did her best to sound nonchalant and not as if her stomach was knotting up, the same awful way it had whenever she'd been faced with a particularly difficult swim meet. To the world, she'd always appeared blasé. Cool under fire. Confident to the nth degree. No one ever knew the hell her insides went through each time. The confidence she radiated only went skin deep. She made sure that she met each challenge, but always, just under the surface, there was the fear that she wouldn't win, that she'd wind up disappointing her father.

She hated disappointing him for a number of reasons. The first because, somewhere in his chauvinistic heart, he had trouble accepting the fact that of his three children, it was his daughter, not his sons who won those medals he so proudly displayed. She wanted to show him that she was just as good as any male, and because to disappoint the colonel meant to leave yourself open for long, long lectures and endless, exhausting training.

The knot in her stomach was identical to the one she felt when she was competing in swim meets and, eventually, Olympic tryouts. Back then she knew why she felt the way she did.

This, however, was something different. Why her stomach now threatened to rise up in her throat, bringing with it everything she'd tasted or eaten in the past twenty-four hours, was completely beyond her. For heaven's sake, she didn't know this man from Adam, why did she even care about his reaction?

He *said* he was her husband. So did her brothers. But the fact that she and this Taylor person had had a relationship didn't mean anything to her beyond being the cause of frustration because she couldn't remember it. None of it. The sensation that there were memories out there that refused to come to her was a little like having an itch just under a layer of scar tissue. Scratching didn't alleviate the itch because she couldn't really feel the contact between nails and skin.

The itch just continued to annoy her.

Just as this did.

"Yeah, I'm home." He raised a piece of the tape.

It gave with the movement, remaining tied. He fought the strong urge just to yank it all away. "What the hell *is* all this?" he asked again.

She was going to be the better person, she told herself. She was going to hang on to her temper even as he lost his. "What does it look like?"

He frowned deeply. Just what did she think she was doing? "Like you're marking off a crime scene."

"No," she said evenly, careful to keep a smile she didn't feel on her face. "I'm dividing up the house." She'd decided that this was the only way for now, if they were going to have to share the same living quarters.

The situation between them was difficult enough to deal with as it was. Having this yellow tape threading its way through what he assumed was every room was like having her thumb her nose at him.

Taylor glared at her. "What the hell for?"

Just as with her father, Gayle had the feeling that backing off from this man just allowed him to run right over you. She wasn't about to be run over. "I'd think that would be obvious."

He wrapped some of the tape around his hand but still managed to refrain from pulling it down. Just barely. "Enlighten me."

She went toe-to-toe with him. "This way we can go around the house without getting in each other's way." She bit back the part about if he were a gentleman, he'd move out until they resolved this, one way or another. She had a feeling that would only set him off and she wasn't trying to argue. She wanted to find a way to coexist in this bizarre situation. "Since you say this is my house and it appears to be your house, as well—"

It had always struck him as uncanny the way she could pluck exactly the wrong word out of the air and annoy the hell out of him. "'Appears'?"

She ignored his tone. "We need a plan for peaceful coexistence. I can't have you coming into my space when I'm getting ready to go to work."

He felt as if he was being baited. "You read scores off a teleprompter," he pointed out. "It's not exactly brain surgery."

There were things she could put up with. Having her job at the station belittled was not one of them. "No, it's certainly not." Sarcasm entered her voice. "Not like swinging a sledgehammer."

Taylor had never had a problem with her being in the spotlight and his standing in the shadows. Self-image had never been something that was shaky with him, even when someone had once referred to him as Mr. Gayle Elliott. He'd always been his own man. But to have her throw a comment like that at him *did* hurt.

"I do a lot more than swing a sledgehammer," he informed her. He almost said "And you know it," except that she didn't, he realized. Not anymore.

He was going to have to tell her this all over again. Tell her that after he'd discovered that he liked changing the face of existing structures, he'd gone to a nearby university at night and gotten his degree in architecture. What he'd learned enabled him to take what was and create something that had never been in the original plans. Something that he felt suited the owners' personalities. Working on houses had turned into a form of art for him.

She didn't let him continue. Instead she fisted her hands at her hips and angrily glared up at him. "And I do a hell of a lot more than read off a teleprompter."

"Yeah, you interview half-naked men in the locker room."

He bit off a curse. What the hell was wrong with him? He didn't mean that. Had he not felt as if his whole world was in danger of falling apart, he would never have said something like that to her, never allowed a comment like that to come out.

But right now there was this desperate feeling in his chest, as if he was trying to cross over an abyss using a bridge made out of oatmeal.

Gayle's blue-green eyes narrowed. Hot words rose in her throat. She took a deep breath. It didn't help. Every time this so-called husband was around her, or even when she thought about him, all her nerve endings rose to the surface.

With effort, she deliberately ignored his last comment. "I divided the kitchen in half. The stove and the refrigerator are in neutral territory."

"Neutral territory," he repeated. He still couldn't believe this was happening. "What is this, a war?"

She drew herself up to her full height. He was still more than half a foot taller than she was. "I don't know, you tell me."

The war part was supposed to be long over with. They'd gotten past that. "Gayle, you're my wife."

He was going to take her in his arms, she sensed it. Gayle took a step back before he could make contact. Something about his touch made her forget things. And she needed to remember, not forget.

"But if I can't remember being your wife, it doesn't count, does it? As far as I'm concerned, you're a complete stranger. An irritating stranger," she added because her feelings still smarted from his terse, unfair summation of her career. "And I don't jump into bed with strangers. Never have, never will."

There, he thought, he had her. "But you did with me."

Almost from the very first moment, sparks had flown between them. As much as they initially attempted to stay away from each other, they couldn't. He found excuses to be where she was, and he suspected she did the same. Within a month, she'd stopped seeing Rico. The very day she told him that she had, they wound up making love. He wasn't even sure who had initiated it. All he knew was that it had happened and that they came very close to incinerating the house he was working on.

It was the first time he'd ever felt lightning surge through his veins.

She sniffed at his statement. Inside she could feel

everything turn to jelly again. She had to put a stop to that.

"According to you."

"Yes, according to me. You can't seem to remember, and I was the only other person there besides you. We didn't exactly take out an ad in the trade papers." He looked at her, his frustration becoming close to unmanageable. "Isn't any of this coming back to you?"

A section of her brain felt as if it was packed in cotton. The section where memories of him undoubtedly resided. What he said could have happened. He certainly had the photographs to prove that they were married.

But she needed more than visual aids. She needed to *feel* they were married, that they were connected. And she didn't. Right now all she felt was adrift. And confused.

Gayle shook her head as she looked into his eyes. "No."

For just a moment she could have sworn she saw a sadness in his eyes. The next moment it was gone, as if some kind of a curtain had gone down, shutting her out.

A hiss of frustration escaped Taylor's lips as he backed away from her. He gestured around at the area with its offending tape. "And you're going to keep this stuff up?"

Because his voice challenged her, she was defiant. "Yes." And then she added, "Until I remember."

He'd had just about all he could take for now. Angrily he crossed back to the front door. "Well, give me a call when you do."

Just for the tiniest part of a moment, a memory flashed across her brain. She tried to capture it in vain. It refused to be summoned back. Exasperation strummed along her soul.

"Where are you going?"

He yanked open the door. She could make him burn up his fuse faster than anyone he knew. "Somewhere where I can get some peace."

Gayle almost ran to the door to stop him, reflexes taking over where there was no thought process involved. *This has happened before,* a voice whispered in her head.

Again she couldn't grasp the memory or even pieces of it.

"I don't have your number," she called after him. But her voice didn't carry above the sound of the slamming door.

Jerk! she thought. She had no idea why she felt like crying.

It didn't hit Taylor that he had no change of clothes until he was a good three blocks away from the house. But he refused to turn back and get them. He would come back and change tomorrow, when he knew she was at the studio.

He had no one to impress where he was going. Hands gripping the wheel, struggling to contain the irritation he felt, both with her and himself, Taylor drove back to the house he was renovating.

To help facilitate working conditions, the owners had both the electricity and the water turned on. So, even though the house looked as if it had suffered through a medium-size earthquake, it was basically livable. He didn't require much. He never had.

As he pulled up in front of the house he'd left not more than an hour ago, he realized that at least he'd done one thing right. He hadn't cleaned out the back of the truck's cab. Which meant that the sleeping bags were still there.

He pulled out his. He and Gayle had taken the truck to the Angeles National Forest last month and gone camping. Roughing it for Gayle meant staying at a motel instead of a hotel, but she did this for him, because he enjoyed it so much.

Taylor paused, remembering that although they'd brought two sleeping bags, they'd wound up in one.

He shook off the memory. Thinking about that now wasn't going to do him any good. Taylor forced himself to focus on the positive. At least he had something to sleep in. If he could sleep.

Which he couldn't.

After approximately four hours of tossing and turning on the hardwood floor, he gave up. The fast-food hamburger that constituted his dinner lay on his stomach like a leaden hockey puck. The fries had been too greasy and threatened to nauseate him. Taylor attributed his sleeplessness to that, though in his heart he knew better.

Knew that it didn't have anything to do with over-cooked food.

He missed her. Missed "them." And more than that, he was beginning to fear that maybe she was never coming back into his life. That they wouldn't be "them" again.

Rolling over, he stared up at the ceiling, watching the moving shadows cast by the full moon weaving through the trees outside the window. Gayle was stubborn enough to keep him at bay, he knew that. And he knew she meant what she'd said. She didn't sleep with strangers. What if she intended to keep him a stranger until her memory came back?

Taylor stared into the empty fireplace beside him, trying to think.

Trying to visualize the rest of his life without Gayle.

He couldn't.

Hell, every time she went away on one of her business trips, he threw himself into his job, working sometimes eighteen hours at a clip because he couldn't face the emptiness in the house without her. Sam and Jake always tried to get him to come out with them, but Gayle's brothers were both bachelors and that life no longer interested him. He didn't want it anymore.

So what were his options? If Gayle had no memory of him...

If she had no memory of him, he was going to have to give her new memories, he decided suddenly. Much as he hated the idea of having to start from scratch again, Sam was right in what he'd said to him this morning. He was going to have to make up his mind to win Gayle all over again.

To "court" her.

Taylor covered his face and groaned. After having enjoyed the delicious intimacies of marriage for the past eighteen months, it was going to be damn hard to go back to square one. To take baby steps until he was finally able to reach the same footing he'd been on just a few days ago. Damn hard.

But then, he didn't have any other option left. Other than to walk away completely, and it went without saying that he would have rather died than do that. Gayle was the center of his world, even though he'd never told her as much. Without her, there was no reason to go on.

Okay, he decided, that was the plan. Pretending that the woman he loved more than anything wasn't his wife but someone he had to win over. He'd done it once, he could do it again. How hard could it be, right?

Taylor frowned. Very hard, as he recalled. Part of the reason was that he'd never had to go out of his way to get companionship before. Women always came on to him. It was a little like living in the middle of an orchard. If he wanted an apple, all he had to do was put out his hand and one all but fell into his palm. With Gayle he'd had to actively pursue her, once he'd made up his mind that he wanted her. The road to the altar had been bumpy, because with Gayle nothing ever went according to plan.

But that was okay. That was what made her Gayle. And desirable.

Taylor lay back down in his sleeping bag. He laced his fingers together and tried to assume a calm pose, willing himself to sleep.

Who the hell was he kidding? he thought three minutes later. He was wired and wide-awake, ready to jump-start his plan. But he knew he wouldn't exactly make any points with her if he turned up at the door at two in the morning.

With a sigh that went down to his very toes, Taylor unzipped the rest of his sleeping bag and got up. He might as well do something productive as he waited for dawn to come.

Twelve hours later found him showered, shaved, changed and walking through the rear of the studio where the Channel Eight local news was taped each day. Just his luck, he ran into several people he recognized, who also recognized him. He was forced to nod a silent greeting at all of them.

He knew them by sight if not by name—he'd never been very good with names—because Gayle had introduced them all at one time. They were all part of what she referred to as the Channel Eight "family."

Did the "family" know? he wondered. As he passed by one of the sound men, he saw the man looking at him. Was that a knowing look or just a curious one?

Damn it, he felt like a fool, but it was too late to turn back now.

The questions continued nagging at him. Had Gayle told people about her accident? About conveniently cutting him out of her memory bank?

"Nice bouquet," a redheaded woman in rimless glasses told him. "She'll love 'em."

God, he hoped so.

As he approached her dressing room, Taylor felt increasingly uneasy. The desire to take flight played tug-of-war with his determination to see this through.

Determination won by a small margin. He'd always been a private person. Living with Gayle had changed all that. There was always someone to take their picture at any of the events they attended. He'd never been happy about that, but he'd done it for her.

Just as she'd put up with camping for him, he reminded himself.

His hand tightened on the flowers he was holding.

If he wanted to continue living with Gayle, he was going to have to let a lot of things ride for the time being.

Gayle took the tiny microphone off of her blouse and removed the earpiece she'd been hooked up to during the broadcast. She'd just finished taping the afternoon installment of the sports news and wasn't needed back until the early evening. Putting both pieces of equipment down on the desk, she said a couple of words to Paul Hunter, the man who did the traffic report, and stepped off the dais.

"Want to get something to eat?" Paul asked eagerly. "No, thanks, I've got a few things to catch up on."

Paul nodded. "See you later, then." As the newest member of their "family," Paul was still trying to find his way.

Aren't we all? she thought cryptically.

About to go to her dressing room, she stopped dead. The man in her wedding photographs was coming toward her. What was he doing here?

She felt her heart flutter and told herself she was getting light-headed because she hadn't eaten. When Taylor stormed out last night, he'd mysteriously taken her appetite with him. She'd had a less than restful night and this morning Julia had commented that for once, she had need of her art to erase the dark circles from beneath Gayle's eyes.

Damn it, he was all right. He'd made her worry for nothing. Even though she couldn't remember him in her life, she didn't want anything happening to him because of her, and she didn't know if he was capable of doing something drastic.

But now that she saw he was in one piece, she felt her anger flaring. After he'd walked out last night, she wasn't sure where they stood. Or even *if* they stood anywhere at all.

Yet even as her heart did a strange little somersault at the sight of him, Gayle could feel herself stiffening inside. Like a warrior about to do battle. She had no explanation for it. God, she wished there was some magic wand that could be waved over her brain and make it come back to normal.

"What's that?" She nodded at his hand.

Taylor glanced at his offering. It was a last-minute thought, pulled up from the garden of the house he was working on. There was no harm in uprooting the flowers, since the owners wanted the garden paved over and covered with stamped, colored concrete.

"Flowers."

"I know they're flowers," she said impatiently. "What are they doing in your hand?"

"Currently?" He studied them for a moment. "Wilting." Taylor thrust the small bouquet toward her. "They're your favorite. White daisies."

She took them with both hands, trying not to let the gesture touch her. "Yes, I know."

"Right." Taylor shoved his hands into his pockets. It was on the tip of his tongue to say something about how she seemed to remember everything but him, but there was no point to it. His job was to create a place for himself in her world. "I was thinking maybe if you're free, we could have lunch."

Shifting the bouquet over to one hand, Gayle looked at her watch. "It's after two."

Taylor dug in, suddenly feeling that if he didn't

make some kind of connection, some kind of break-through soon, he might never be able to. He needed to make just one step forward, just one.

"A late lunch. An early dinner. Something on a plate, doesn't matter what we call it. Just come out with me."

She looked down at the bouquet for a second. She'd always loved daisies. They were so light, so free. "I have to get back by four-thirty."

"Is that a no?"

"No." She let a smile curve her lips. "That's a time limit."

Taylor smiled for the first time in almost three days. "Okay, then. I can work with that." About to take her hand, he stopped. "Do you mind?"

His thoughtfulness surprised her. And pleased her. "No," she said quietly, "I don't mind."

She told herself it was only static electricity that shot through her when they touched.

Chapter Eight

"So what's the occasion?"

Gayle had to raise her voice a little in order to be heard once they were seated. She'd opted to go to the restaurant she frequented most often. It was convenient because it was located a block and a half from the studio, and the food was decent enough.

Obviously, a lot of other people felt the same way. Although the lunch crunch was almost over, Monroe's was still doing a brisk amount of business. Three-quarters of the tables were filled with people who either worked somewhere in the immediate area or had shopped till they dropped.

Taylor looked at her. In general, he found a lot of

Gayle's questions to be enigmatic, but now that she thought they were strangers, he felt really lost, without a compass to guide him.

"What do you mean?"

Gayle opened the menu just to see if anything new had been added. The owner operated on the principle that if it worked, don't fix it, and for the most part the selections on the menu worked.

"The flowers you brought," she prompted.

He began to wonder if maybe the scans done at the hospital had missed something. Was her short-term memory going, too?

Taylor didn't bother opening the menu. Instead he tucked it off to the side. "I thought we already had this conversation."

She paused to smile at the approaching waitress. They knew her here and treated her as if she were family rather than a celebrity. She liked that. "No, it stopped somewhere around when you said they were wilting. The next thing you said were that they were my favorites."

"Right."

"I'll have the Black Forest ham sandwich on rye. Mustard, no mayo. Lettuce, green pepper. Diet cola," she told the waitress who made a couple of squiggles on her pad, then turned toward Taylor.

"Same," he echoed, surrendering his menu to the young woman.

"But why did you bring them?" Gayle pressed, the moment the waitress retreated. "The flowers," she repeated in case he'd lost the thread amid the din and the sandwich order.

Gayle's question took Taylor back to the early days of their relationship, before trust had entered the picture. He'd almost forgotten this habit of hers. Gayle used to view almost everything remotely personal as suspicious. He supposed that was her defense mechanism.

People were always trying to curry her favor in exchange for a favor in return. And, if he correctly recalled some of the stories she later confided to him, Gayle felt that almost each and every time her father was nice to her, he was trying to get her to agree to something she'd already turned down. Like another competition, or a product endorsement she'd taken a pass on. Until shortly after the last Olympics, her father had not only been her coach but her manager, as well. She'd declared her independence from the colonel just shortly before they began going out together.

For a while Taylor got the feeling that by being with him Gayle was afraid she'd jumped out of the frying pan into the fire. It had taken a great deal of patience on his part to convince her that not only was he not interested in her money, he wanted to use only his when it came to buying things for them. As far as he was concerned, she could bank hers or use it for charity. He was the breadwinner. She'd balked, then agreed.

The waitress materialized with their sodas, then, flashing a smile, retreated again.

He countered her question with a question. "Why does anyone bring flowers to a woman?"

Her eyes met his. "To get something."

He thought for a moment before giving her a response. "I suppose, in a way, you're right."

He saw her stiffen ever so slightly. Someone else might have missed that, but he was keenly aware of every nuance, every gesture that went into making Gayle the woman she was. "And what is it that you want to get?"

He could have cut the suspicion emanating from her with a knife. "Into your favor."

She tossed her hair over her shoulder. It was a movement she did when she felt as if she'd pinned someone down. "And into other places?"

There was no point in denying that. It was his ultimate goal. To have her as his wife again. "Eventually. When you remember me."

"And if I don't?" she asked. "If my memory of you never comes back, what then?"

He snapped off a piece of the garlic breadstick he snared from the small basket in the middle of the table and took a bite before answering. "Then I'm going to make you want to remember me."

The guy was good-looking. More than good-looking, and she had to admit a current buzzed between them. But she absolutely hated egotists. She found it hard to believe that she'd actually married one.

"Pretty confident in yourself, aren't you?"

His eyes held hers for a long moment. So long that she felt something scrambling in her stomach, and she was fairly certain it wasn't hunger pangs. At least, not for food.

His voice was low, seductive, as he leaned forward and said, "Let's just say that in this one instance, I believe in history repeating itself."

She did what she could to cut him dead. The smile on her lips was icy. "And you swept me off my feet the first time around, right?"

Taylor laughed shortly. Despite the surrounding din, the sound seeped into her bones.

"Nobody sweeps you off your feet, Gayle. But I did manage to lift you off the ground a couple of inches." Was that humor he saw flirting with the corners of her mouth? Or was it just that sly, cynical look that sometimes came over her face? At the outset it was hard to tell. He was rooting for the former. "No more than you did me," he added.

Gayle stared at him, his meaning momentarily lost on her. She sincerely doubted he was saying what it sounded like he was saying. "No more than I did you, what?"

Taylor took a breath. It wasn't easy for him to make these kinds of personal admissions. He wasn't the kind to put his feelings into words, or bare his soul. He'd always been pretty closemouthed. But he knew that if he continued that way, he stood to lose the reason he had any feelings at all.

"Dissolve the ground beneath my feet." He

paused for a second, a soldier attempting to regroup after his buddies had disappeared on him. "I thought we could start from scratch."

He looked damn uncomfortable. Suddenly she wasn't any longer. She was enjoying herself. Gayle leaned her chin on the palm of her propped-up hand and looked at him. "And just what is it you'd be scratching?"

To the untrained ear, she might have sounded seductive. But he knew better. Knew her inside and out and yet she still managed to surprise him on more than just a few occasions.

I miss you, damn it. Come back to me, Gayle.

"Stop being so damn suspicious, Gayle," he said aloud. "In case you haven't noticed, I'm trying my best here to court you."

"Court me." She repeated the term incredulously. "I don't know you—"

How many times were they going to rehash this? "That's just the problem."

Gayle continued as if he hadn't interrupted her. He'd missed her meaning entirely. "But you don't strike me as the kind of man who normally uses the word *court*. If ever," she added.

Damn it, how did this always happen? How did she manage to twist things around so that he lost sight of his original meaning, his original goal? Did she take delight in confounding him like this, even if she couldn't remember him?

"Maybe it's because I don't know what other

word to use." Realizing that he was very close to shouting, Taylor made an effort to lower his voice. Taking a second to regain control over his close-to-frayed temper, he decided he might as well tell her everything. It was better that way. Safer. Gayle had an uncanny knack of finding things out, anyway. "Besides, it was Sam's word."

The waitress returned again, this time with their food. She quickly placed a plate before each of them, then hurried off to another couple that had just been seated. "And why would my five-alarm brother be saying the word *court* around you?"

It probably would have gone better for him if he took credit for the idea. But he'd never believed in lies, even ones that placed him in a better light. Lies were far too difficult to keep track of. He had no idea how Sam managed to juggle as many as he did.

"Because that was what he suggested I do with you." Then, because she seemed so eager to believe the worst, he said cryptically, "Me, I'd just as soon tie you up, throw you over my shoulder and take you off to some secluded lair until you finally came to your senses."

Gayle looked down at the sandwich she was holding. Absorbed in the image he'd just created, she'd all but squeezed it flat in the middle. She made a conscious effort to relax her fingers, at the same time eyeing him darkly. "Now *that* sounds like you."

He figured he'd put up with just about enough. She was far too willing to cast him in the role of a Ne-

The Reader Service™ — Here's how it works:

NO STAMP NEEDED!

THE READER SERVICE™
FREE BOOK OFFER
FREEPOST CN81
CROYDON
CR9 3WZ

NO STAMP
NECESSARY
IF POSTED IN
THE U.K. OR N.I.

anderthal, and he resented it. "How would you know?"

How would she know? The question echoed in her brain like a bell sounded at vespers. She had no answer for that, at least, not for herself. But she wasn't about to let him know that. If you didn't have all the answers, people tried to give you theirs, and suddenly you were no more than an extension of them.

The way the colonel had always fought to make her an extension of himself. Had she not been blessed with a will of iron, she would have long ago been plowed under by the very father who loved her.

Gayle shrugged nonchalantly. "Instinct."

He came very close to throwing up his hands and just walking out of the restaurant. But walking away meant he'd be alone. Without her. And he'd already danced that dance. He was in this for the long haul, ready to do whatever it took. He'd had a life with Gayle and without Gayle—and with was definitely better.

"Gayle, I'm trying here. Work with me."

What had her marriage been like? Had he made her surrender pieces of herself without realizing it until it was too late? Was that why she couldn't remember him? There had to be a reason. There *had* to be. But if that was the reason, she knew he wouldn't tell her. She was on her own here.

Gayle looked at him for a long moment. "And what's in it for me?"

He wanted to shout at her that she'd asked an absurd question. But he knew her, knew the old Gayle before she'd become *his* Gayle. And the old Gayle thought that way. Because she was afraid of being caught off guard. Afraid of being vulnerable.

"At the risk of sounding vain...me," he answered. "And our marriage."

Okay, she would put the question to him just to see what his answer would be. Not that she expected him to be honest, but it might be entertaining to watch him squirm. "If our marriage was so special, why did I forget it? Why did I forget you?"

"That's something we need to find out." Taylor placed his hand over hers, then turned it over and held it for a moment. He had to admit he was a little surprised as well as gratified that she didn't pull away. "We can't do it if you keep fighting me at every turn."

The smile that emerged on her lips was soft.

A little bit of hope burrowed through his heart.

"I can't help it," she told him. "It's what I do."

It was a moment, a tiny moment, but he cherished it. "I know. But maybe if you fight just a little less, we might get somewhere."

Under the pretext of getting back to eating her lunch, she separated her hand from his.

"Okay." And then, just as she bit into her sandwich, a question occurred to her. She raised her eyes to his. "Does this mean that you're moving back in?"

"I didn't exactly move out. All I had were the clothes on my back," he reminded her. "But yes, I'm back in."

She chewed on his answer as she ate her lunch. "All right," she agreed gamely, her stomach unaccountably fluttering. "But the tape stays up."

Every time he thought he was making the slightest bit of headway, she'd turn around and come up with a way to negate it. "Gayle…"

Raising an index finger in the air, she didn't let him finish his protest. "If you were 'courting' me," Gayle said, struggling to suppress a laugh, "you'd be living in your own apartment."

"House," he corrected. He'd been living in houses ever since he'd begun renovating them.

"Whatever," she allowed, "and I'd be living in mine. But since we both obviously live in that hollowed-out shell, having the rooms separated with tape is the next best thing."

There was nothing "best" about having to face yellow police tape snaking its way through every room, Taylor thought grudgingly. But if that was the only way to get her to live in the same house with him, so be it. He had no choice but to agree to her terms, because he needed the proximity in order to make his plan work. As far as plans went, it was a very simple one. If he couldn't make Gayle remember that there was a place for him in her heart, then he was just going to have to create one there all over again.

He just hoped he was up to it.

Placing what was left of her sandwich on her plate, Gayle put her hand out to him. "Do we have a deal?"

Her eyes were on his face. As if she could gauge if he was telling the truth or not by watching his expression. She didn't remember how well he could play poker, he thought. She really didn't remember him at all.

The thought hit home for the dozenth time. And still hurt just as much as it had the first time.

Taylor absolutely hated this position he found himself in. Hated having to go through these charades. Hated having her look at him and know that she wasn't seeing him the way she'd come to see him. That the full spectrum of the past eighteen months they'd shared had completely vanished from her memory and now only existed in his.

It was almost like being a widower.

But, damn it, he was going to bring his wife back from the dead.

Taylor wrapped his strong fingers around the hand that was held out to him. "Deal."

It took her a minute to disengage her hand from his. Just for the slightest fleeting moment, as his fingers had joined with hers, she'd experienced a sensation she couldn't quite label. She'd felt…safe, for lack of a better term.

But that was just an illusion, and she knew better than to give in to it. If anything it made her feel utterly unsafe the very next moment.

She threaded her fingers together, forming a bridge before her. "Just so you know," she told him sweetly, "I'll cut your heart out if you try anything underhanded."

Damn, here was the spirit that had first attracted him. The spirit that kept reeling him in when it was smarter to swim in the opposite direction.

"What about the old expression," he posed, "'all's fair in love and war'?"

She waved a hand, dismissing the sentiment. "Coined by an old eunuch."

And she was probably the one who had done the honors, he thought. This was going to be one hell of a challenge.

An unexpected late-summer shower had cast the world into premature shades of darkness and gray by the time he returned to the house he was working on. Because of his mood, Taylor made do with very little illumination. There was just enough to allow him to see what he was doing and no more.

When Jake found him, he commented that Batman had more light in his cave than was presently available here.

"I like it dark," Taylor all but growled as he took one final pass with his sander along the bottom of the door laid out across two sawhorses. The fit was still a bit too snug. Real muscle had to be applied to the door in order to open or close it. The owners weren't paying him to set up wrestling matches with wood each time they wanted to enter or exit the house.

"I take it that things aren't going well on the home front. Sam told me about his suggestion."

Retiring his sander, Taylor looked up at him. "She likes the idea."

"Terrific. I had a feeling she might come around when he mentioned it to me." And then Jake paused, reading his brother-in-law's expression. "But, correct me if I'm wrong, you're less than thrilled about this."

"She's my wife, Jake. It'll feel weird treating her like a girlfriend."

Jake grinned. "At least you're not walking into something blindly. Most guys have no idea if they're compatible with the girl they're going out with. You already know a lot of things ahead of time."

"Yeah, like she's got a mean left hook once she gets angry," Taylor muttered, cleaning off the area he'd just sanded.

"That's the kind of thing I'm talking about," Jake laughed. He stepped around so that Taylor could see him. "Look, think of it as a way of breathing new life into your marriage."

"My marriage had plenty of life," Taylor retorted. "Sorry," he apologized the next minute.

His detective brother-in-law seemed not to hear him. He was obviously still exploring what he'd just said. "A lot of guys start taking their wives for granted. Having to win her all over again will shake things up for you."

That was the last thing he needed. "Things are already shaken up," Taylor pointed out. "And what makes you such a walking expert on marriage, anyway?" he asked, dusting off his hands. "Your longest relationship lasted six weeks."

"Nine," Jake corrected. "And a lot of the guys on the force are married." The locker room was a regular bull pen of grievances and complaints, whether it was about wives or live-in girlfriends. "It sounds like once they say 'I do,' they don't."

Taylor didn't quite follow. "Don't what?"

Jake looked down at the door still lying across the sawhorses. The front had simple but decorative carving on it. "Nice work."

"Thanks. You were saying? Don't what?" Taylor repeated.

"Don't enjoy themselves anymore with the woman they promised to love and cherish."

Taylor knew the statistics. Knew that half the marriages these days ended up in divorce. People took the easy way out rather than sticking it out and fighting for their marriage. His mouth curved. Gayle certainly had the fighting part down pat.

"It wasn't like that with Gayle and me."

Jake knew that. As the months of her marriage went by, he'd noticed a new calmness about his sister that he'd never seen before. He figured it had to do with living with Taylor.

"All the more reason to get her to come around again." He paused, the detective in him coming out. "Does seem funny, though, her losing her memory of you. Blanking out about the accident is normal. A lot of people suffer from shock after something like that and they block out what their subconscious feels is a life-threatening event."

He looked at Taylor. "But to forget someone like a husband... Have you figured out what might have prompted her to do that?"

"If I did, you'd be the first to know," Taylor said. "You wanna give me a hand with this?"

"Sure, where do you want it?"

"Over by the entrance." He picked up the end closest to him.

Jake picked up the other end of the door and started walking backward to the doorway. As he got closer, he could feel the raindrops coming in through the open space. Jake decided to press his point a little more.

"Everything between the two of you okay?" Taylor raised his eyes from the surface of the door they were carrying to his face. "I'm asking as a friend, not as her brother."

"Okay, 'friend,'" Taylor replied evenly. He knew Jake was just being concerned and while he would rather have kept all of this to himself, he did appreciate the support he knew was there. "Everything between us was fine." He set the door upright. "Hold it steady for me," he instructed as he began to put the two bolts back in place. "Oddly enough, given Gayle's love of combat, there were no knock-down, drag-out arguments preceding her mental holiday. Things were going great. She looked a little off," he recalled, "but she said it was because of all the road trips she'd put in during the previous month." Finished, he stepped back to survey his work. "You can let go now." Jake did as he was told. "Hell," Taylor said, "we were even talking about having a family."

"What? That's great." And then Jake paused, looking at his brother-in-law, not quite sure of what he was seeing. "That is great, isn't it?"

"Yeah," Taylor allowed. "Eventually. Not right now, though. She loves her job and I want to get some more money into the bank before we have a baby."

Jake looked at him incredulously. Gayle had been raking in endorsements ever since she'd won her first Olympics at seventeen. And the colonel had turned out to be a pretty shrewd investor. There was no lack of funds as far as Gayle was concerned. "Tay—"

Taylor held up his hand, knowing exactly where Jake was going. "Yeah, I know, she's got a lot of money. But if we're having kids, *I* want to be the one who earns it. At least a sizable chunk of it," he amended. "I'm old-fashioned that way."

Jake grinned, shaking his head. He'd always liked Taylor. He'd known he was a man of integrity right from the start.

"Who'd have thunk it?" He crossed his arms before him. "What did Gayle say?"

"She agreed," Taylor said simply.

Jake's eyebrows drew together. "She didn't fight you on it, not even for principle's sake?"

"No."

Jake's puzzled expression deepened. "Doesn't sound like Gayle."

Taylor nodded. "That's what I mean. She was finally mellowing out a little." He sighed. "And now I'm back to square one."

Jake put his arm around his shoulders. He was older than his brother-in-law by two years. And exactly the same height. "You'll make it, buddy. In the meantime this'll get the old juices flowing."

"Thanks, Dear Abby." Taylor laughed dryly as he stepped back. "I'll try to remember that."

"Hey, it could be worse."

"How?" Taylor wanted to know. "How could it possibly be any worse than having your wife forget who you are?"

"She could remember," Jake teased, tongue-in-cheek, "and hate the sight of you."

This time Taylor really did laugh. It helped knock off a little of the tension. "I guess you've got a point there."

Jake took the tool that Taylor had just picked up out of his hand. "Don't you have a little woman to be heading home to?"

"If she hears you call her that, you'll be the one

without a memory. Because she will have ripped your head off."

Jake grinned. "She is mild tempered, my little sister." And then his expression sobered just a little. "Hang in there, Taylor."

"Have to," Taylor told him. "I don't have any other choice."

From the moment he first saw her, standing beside Rico and laughing at something the quarterback was saying, he knew that there was no other choice for him but Gayle. And if the road was bumpy sometimes, well, that just made him appreciate the smooth times that much more.

Chapter Nine

As he approached the house, he saw there were no lights on. Granted it was only 6:00 in the evening and this was summer, but the inside of the house tended to be dark. Part of his plan was to put skylights in the living room and the family room to allow more sunshine into the house.

Uneasiness descended over him as he scanned the outside of the building, looking for a glimmer to indicate she was home. Today was her early day. Someone else covered the sports on the evening news.

Her car was gone. Was she just out somewhere or had she abruptly decided to leave? And if it was the latter, where did he go to look for her? He had no idea where to start.

The silence that greeted him as he entered was deafening and eerie. Taylor closed the door behind him, feeling as if he was sealing himself in a tomb.

She was supposed to be here, he thought irritably. They were supposed to spend the evening together. This "courting" thing was going awfully slowly. He'd been at it for over a week, and the more time they spent together, the more chances he had at getting her to remember him. And love him all over again.

Parched and angry, he strode into the kitchen to get a drink of water. Which was when he saw it. A note, written on shopping-list paper and posted with a magnet in the shape of a baseball pennant on the refrigerator.

Taylor,
Forgot I had a night game to go to. Go Angels!
Gayle.

That was it. No real salutation, no small heart drawn at the end of the note the way she always closed her notes to him. Nothing.

He supposed he should be happy that she'd at least let him know where she was. When they were first going out, she'd balked at that. Said it felt too confining to her. The note was a concession.

He didn't feel very happy.

Taylor crumpled the note and tossed it in the general direction of the garbage pail. He missed, and the misshapen paper ball fell on the floor. Muttering under his breath, he went to retrieve it.

There was a length of yellow tape right in front of the garbage pail. Taylor ripped it away, uttering a few words he rarely said.

Saying them didn't make him feel any better.

He picked up the crumpled paper and shoved it into the garbage. Damn it, what was he doing, chasing his tail and trying to recapture the past? He sure as hell didn't need this. But he did need Gayle, and the sooner he stopped letting his temper flare up and get the better of him, the sooner he could reach his end goal.

He *had* to reach end goal, he thought. Had to win her over.

Although he could think of a lot better ways to spend his evening than watching a bunch of grown men waving highly polished sticks at oncoming spheres traveling up to a hundred miles an hour, he was going to the game. Because that was where Gayle was.

All he had to do was find out where the game was being held. He prayed it wasn't an away game.

The newspaper was still sitting on the breakfast counter, its sections haphazardly pulled apart. The sports section was right on top.

Taylor smiled to himself as he crossed to the counter. Apparently her habits hadn't changed. At least the ones that didn't involve him, he thought grudgingly.

He began rifling through the sports section, vaguely remembering that the times and places for all the games being played today were written somewhere in the front.

He wasn't much for sports. The truth of it was he was only marginally aware of the names of the teams domiciled in California. He wouldn't have known even that if it hadn't been for Gayle. Early in their relationship, after she'd gotten over the horror of finding out that he didn't follow sports, she'd attempted to indoctrinate him about the various teams and the rules that went with each game. Most of what she'd told him had barely sunk in and was ready to be dislodged by the introduction of any new, minor passing fact.

He'd never been a joiner, so team sports were the last thing he paid attention to when he was growing up. And he never had the need or desire to live life vicariously, so turning on his set to watch a game never occurred to him. He followed no team until there was Gayle. Because it was so important to her and because sports played such a significant part in her world, he tried to work up an interest.

Although she tried to sound impartial when she was talking about a game on the news, anyone with eyes could see that she fairly glowed whenever she could report that one of her teams had won. What Gayle cared about, she cared about passionately. There was no middle ground with her.

She was the same with people. Having been on

the receiving end of her passion this last year and a half, he was acutely aware of its lack. He needed to be on the receiving end of it as much as he needed to breathe.

Most of all, he needed her to look at him the way she had before the accident.

The information he was seeking was on the left-hand side of page four. Skimming down the page he saw that the Angels were playing a home game. Taylor stared at the information, thinking. And then he remembered. Home for the Angels meant the stadium in Anaheim, not the one in Los Angeles. That was where the Dodgers played. Any five-year-old kid in Southern California probably knew that, but for him it was a breakthrough.

He folded the paper, leaving it in a neat pile, and glanced at his watch. According to the paper, the game was scheduled to begin just after five, which meant it was already in progress. He'd missed kick-off.

No, he amended, that was a football term. What the hell did they call it when they started a baseball game?

Boring, a small voice whispered in his head.

But boring or not, that was where Gayle was, so that was where he was going to be. Besides, since it was after six, he wouldn't have to sit through the whole thing, and he could make points with her for going to the game.

With his luck, the game would probably go into extra innings.

* * *

Gayle wasn't conscious of wrapping her arms around herself as she watched the field. The Angels were due up at bat. She could feel excitement radiating through her body.

God, but she loved the great American pastime. Yes, she loved swim meets and the thrill of covering the Olympics, but for sheer exhilaration, nothing beat watching a good baseball game.

This, sadly, did not fall under that heading. But there was still time to rally, and she was an eternal optimist. After the winning season the team had had in 2002, she firmly believed that anything was possible.

Gayle tensed up as the batter came up to the plate. When she was rooting for a team, she felt every swing, every hit, every miss. She cheered, audibly or otherwise, when it was a hit and agonized, secretly or otherwise, when it was not.

She'd been doing a lot of agonizing during this game. Her beloved team was losing eight to one and it was the bottom of the eighth. The Angels had been hitless for six of those innings.

Jack Reyes sat at her left. He was the sportscaster from a rival station and only invested himself in a game if he had a side bet riding on the outcome. Or to rub someone's nose in it.

His thin lips drew back as he gave her a grin that involved not only his teeth, but his gums, as well.

"Looks like you're going to have to pay up, Elliott," Jack crowed. He rubbed his thumb over his fingers several times, indicating that she might as well separate the bills from her wallet now.

Goaded by his smart remarks about the rather infamous way the Angels had of sometimes folding just when they looked as if they would win, Gayle had bet Jack fifty dollars that the Angels would win. It wasn't the money, but the principle that was at stake. Not to mention a chance at the play-offs.

Gayle sniffed and gave the small, thin man a scathing look. "Truest words Yogi Berra ever said were, 'It ain't over till it's over.' So don't start counting those dollar bills just yet, Reyes."

Reyes snorted. "Yeah well, no disrespect to the man but this game is definitely over." He gestured toward the playing field directly outside the plate-glass window surrounding the press box. "Your guys look like they're batting flies—insects, not balls," he added with an even wider grin.

Annoyed, protective, Gayle was about to say something to put Reyes in his place, reminding him that the team had managed to come back from behind so many times it was practically their hallmark, but she never got the chance. Her attention was drawn to the tall, muscular African-American security guard who was entering from the back of the booth. The man never hesitated but came straight to her.

Now what? she wondered.

Towering a good foot over her, the man raised his

eyebrows slightly, as if not a hundred percent sure he had the right person. "Ms. Elliott?"

"Yes?" She was aware that all eyes in the booth had turned in her direction.

"There's a guy out here claiming to be your husband," the guard told her politely. "He says that he wants to see you."

A movement on the field had her attention immediately being redirected to the batter who had just come up to the plate. It was strike one. Gayle waved a dismissive hand toward the guard at her left. "Just someone trying to get into the press box. I don't have a husband."

The guard nodded, moving his hat forward on his clean-shaven head. "Thought so. Sorry to bother you." He began to retreat.

At her statement Reyes immediately snapped to attention and looked at her with new interest. "You get a divorce?"

"No, I—" And then it came back to her. Taylor. The wedding photographs. "Oh, wait," she cried, swinging around. "Wait," she repeated, raising her voice. The security guard stopped by the rear entrance. "What does this guy say his name is?"

"Taylor Conway."

She nodded. She'd forgotten. Again. "Yes, he's my husband."

Reyes frowned. He glanced at her hand. She was still wearing her wedding ring. "Sure doesn't leave much of an impression on you, does he?"

But he does, she thought. That was the weird part. Every time she thought about the way he'd kissed her, she could feel her body tingling, responding like Pavlov's dogs at the sound of the bell.

"It's a long story." She stiffened slightly as she saw Taylor following the guard into the press box.

She glanced at the field, but the batter, one of their better players, had just gotten another strike. The count was 0 and 2. Mentally she crossed her fingers as she hurried over to Taylor and the guard.

"He's mine," she confirmed. "Thanks." His expression never changing, the guard touched the tip of his cap with two fingers and then retreated. Gayle turned to look at Taylor. "What are you doing here?"

Taylor shrugged carelessly. He was supposed to have been here earlier. But evening rush hour traffic had eaten away at his time. What should have taken him fifteen minutes had turned into more than an hour. He was glad there was still some game left to share with her.

"I thought I'd catch the game—and you—in person. It's not against the rules," he told her, in case she was thinking of sending him away on a technicality. "I've been in the press box before."

She cocked her head, studying him. "You like baseball?" Everyone she knew liked the game, but something distant and nebulous prompted her to ask, as if she somehow sensed that he didn't care for sports. If that was true, how could she have married him? She had no answers. Only questions. Lots and lots of questions.

Since she didn't remember him and thus couldn't know that about him, Taylor decided to tip the scales a little in his favor.

"Sure," he said glibly, "who doesn't?"

"Full count," the announcer's voice came over the loud speaker.

Her head swung back toward the field. "Full count," she repeated, stunned. She'd only looked away for a minute. "How did that happen?"

"The pitcher must have thrown him some balls." Taylor figured that was a safe enough comment to make. To his relief, it earned him a fleeting smile before she looked back on the field.

So far, so good, he thought. He'd taken back an inch. Now he needed the rest of the mile.

"Must have," she agreed. A cheer rose up from the stadium and her head swung back toward the field. "What'd I miss? What'd I miss?" she cried. Reyes said something to answer her echoed question, but his words were drowned out by Gayle's cheer as her brain processed what had happened. "A home run! Atta boy, Anderson!" The longtime Angel was proudly rounding the bases.

Blowing out a breath, Gayle turned her attention to the man on her right.

"Why don't you grab a seat?" She nodded toward the far corner where a few folding chairs were clumped together.

"Okay."

One chair leaned into another, almost like drunken revelers trying to stay upright. It took a little finagling to separate them. By the time Taylor claimed a chair, brought it over and started to unfold it, another Angel had hit another home run. And Gayle had leaped to her feet, and maybe a few inches off the ground as well, cheering. Color rose to her cheeks.

The only time she had ever looked more alive than this moment was when they were making love, Taylor caught himself thinking. A pang zipped through his body, making him long for her.

"Hungry?" she asked, barely turning her face toward him, her eyes glued to the field. "There's food behind you." She didn't even bother gesturing toward it, fairly certain she'd wind up hitting someone. She talked with her hands, and once or twice before, the back of her hand had made contact with someone's face.

"C'mon, c'mon," she urged the next batter after he'd let three pitches pass, earning him the count of one ball and two strikes, none of which he'd tried to connect with.

"No, I'm fine," Taylor answered. Food was the last thing on his mind. As he watched, Gayle jumped to her feet, then sank down again when the hit that had looked so perfect had yielded a foul ball.

"Actually, I'm hungry," she told him, her eyes never leaving the batter.

He wasn't sure if that was just a statement, or a barely veiled hint. Okay, he could play the dutiful husband, even if she didn't think of him in those terms yet.

Besides, he recalled, there'd been plenty of times when the tables had been turned and Gayle had served him. Even if she hadn't cooked the meal herself. He thought of a picnic basket filled to capacity with his favorite dishes. She'd brought the basket out to him when he was working to convert an old carriage house into a second home on an estate-size lot in Tustin. That was during the early days of their marriage.

He'd fallen behind schedule and was trying to finish the job in order not to be faced with paying a penalty according to his contract. Some days he worked from dawn to way after dark, putting in sixteen, eighteen hours to finish something.

Gayle had appeared with the basket on her arm, looking far more delectable than anything she could have possibly packed. They'd eaten off a tablecloth on the floor and then made love on it.

He forced himself to bank down the memory. He couldn't deal with it right now. Instead he glanced back at the table. There seemed to be an endless variety of things to choose from. "What'll you have?"

"Hmm?" Eyes riveted to the batter, she had to replay Taylor's words in her head before she understood what he was asking. "Oh, a hot dog'll do fine. Make that two. And no—"

"Ketchup," he finished the sentence for her. "Yes, I know."

I know everything about you. What makes you laugh. What makes you cry. How you hate ketchup on anything and only like one kind of pickle.

That was supposed to make things easier for him, he told himself. Knowing what pitfalls to avoid with her. But it didn't make things easier, not really. Every time he caught her looking at him, that distant, slightly confused look in her eyes, it felt as if someone had punched him straight in the gut. It was particularly hard to breathe then.

Taylor focused on what he was doing.

The buffet table had enough food still on it to feed a small third-world nation. The sportscasters and sportswriters had availed themselves of a lot, but still a great deal was left over. The hot dogs were just that, hot as they made regular passes on an upright rotisserie that kept them ready for consumption. He took two for her, one for himself, housing each in a bun and spreading mustard liberally over each. He used to be a big fan of ketchup, but Gayle had weaned him off the condiment. More by example than anything else. It had just happened.

Just like falling in love with Gayle had just "happened."

Returning to the folding chair, he handed Gayle her paper plate with both hot dogs on it. She took them without looking, her attention glued to the man at the plate. He knew better than to say anything.

The Angels got three men on base in quick succession before going on to collect two outs. Things in the press booth grew tense. This was an important game. If the Angels lost it, they were out of the running for the play-offs.

Instead of watching the game, Taylor watched Gayle. The planes and angles of her face were completely rigid as she followed the movements of the batter at the plate. When the announcer declared that the player was up to a full count, Taylor was certain that Gayle had stopped breathing.

She continued to hold her breath as the batter made contact with the next three balls. All three were fouls.

Just when it looked as if the batter was going to continue hitting foul balls all night, his bat met the next ball and a resounding "crack" was heard throughout the stadium, amplified a hundred times over by the microphones.

Gayle was on her feet the second she heard the sound, screaming and cheering as she willed the ball over the fence.

And then it did just that—flew right over the corner of the back fence, missing the foul line by a hairsbreadth.

"A grand slam!" she cried. "He got a grand slam."

The next second, Gayle was throwing her arms around him. And then her mouth made contact with his. He was aware of tasting just the tiniest bit of mustard before his senses rose to another, more exhilarated level.

The sheer energy he felt was incredible.

Taylor needed no further encouragement. Pulling her to him, his paper plate falling to the floor, he wrapped his arms around her as he deepened the kiss she had initiated.

The adrenaline rush she experienced was overwhelming. By the time Gayle finally broke away, she was literally gasping for air.

Blinking, she looked at Taylor with new admiration. And something more.

He was instantly alert, the euphoric buzz sustained from the kiss moved to the back burners.

"What is it?" he asked. "Did you just remember something?"

"Yes," she whispered, unconsciously touching her fingertips to her lips as she looked at him. "Something."

But what that "something" was she couldn't tell. It was gone before assuming a shape or leaving a clue. In its place was only a by-now-familiar frustration. She shook her head.

"Sorry, I—"

Her apology was drowned out by another wild cheer from the stands. The next player up had just hit a home run and the crowd was going crazy.

"Eight to seven. No doubt about it, folks. These Angels love their miracles," the announcer cried.

They weren't the only ones, Taylor thought, watching Gayle. He could still feel the impact of her lips on his. And she'd remembered something.

Memories of him, of them, were trying to come back to her.

It was a start.

"Eleven to eight, after trailing behind eight to one for eight innings. Looks like our boys in red love doing things the hard way," Gayle said to the camera, visualizing viewers in their living rooms as she spoke. A camera was far too impersonal a piece of equipment. She did her best with living, breathing audiences. When there as none available, she used her imagination. "But in the end, all that counts is the final score. And the heart that went into playing the game."

As the camera swung away, Gayle breathed a happy sigh. Her team had gone on to play another day. There was another World Series pennant in the offing, she could smell it. They just had to get there.

Her eyes shifted to the man standing in the wings. Taylor.

Her pulse quickened again, the memory of the fiery kiss in the press box returned to her with full force.

The man sure knew how to kiss, she thought. One would think she'd remember that kind of thing. That just the act of kissing him would bring it all back to her in spades.

Maybe if she didn't try so hard, it would come back to her. She knew that when she'd finally relaxed a little instead of doing her damnedest to make her father proud of her, she'd started winning the meets she'd competed in. Maybe it was the same with memories. Maybe they came back to you if you didn't try so hard to *make* them come back.

Warmth and tension slipped over her at the same time as Taylor joined her.

"Ready to go home?" he asked.

They'd already gone out with several members of the team after the game, to share a few beers and make a few grandiose toasts, all of which referred to the swiftly approaching World Series. She'd noticed Taylor had remained quiet, letting her hold court. Was that the way of it, she wondered. Was she the dominant one in this marriage she couldn't remember?

After an hour they'd all gone their separate ways. The players to rest up for the next game and she to the studio, to tape a segment for the nightly news. Taylor had quietly hung around the studio, waiting for her to finish. She knew that couldn't have been fun for him.

As he approached her now, he seemed tired and wound up at the same time. Same as her, Gayle thought.

For once she felt no inclination to hold him off with words, or to get into a discussion over his presumption of her state. Despite the odd humming going on in her body, which she stubbornly attributed as a side effect of her overtired state, she didn't feel like challenging him on any level. If anything, she felt rather agreeable.

"Yes," she told him. "I'm ready to go home."

Chapter Ten

Taylor was on his way out the door and to the rest of his day when he glanced at his wristwatch. It was purely out of habit rather than need. He had more than a vague sense of the time. For the most part, he possessed the finely tuned gift of punctuality, of gauging everything properly so that, barring some unforeseen, whimsical act of God, he was never late.

So it wasn't the time registered on the dark-blue face of his watch that threw him; it was the date that was displayed just above the number six.

September 3.

The day he'd proposed to her.

Gayle was only a few steps behind him. Breakfast had consisted of half a bagel and a full cup of black coffee. It was all she needed. Unlike him, she was in danger of running late this morning. She was on her way to an early-morning interview with the manager of the Red Sox. The team had arrived in town late last night, and she had managed to wangle an exclusive interview.

"Something wrong?" she asked as she ran her fingertips first over the lobe of one ear, then the other, checking to see if her earrings were properly fastened.

Taylor didn't move. He stood frozen in the doorway as if someone had waved a magic wand over him.

Gayle suppressed a sigh. She still wasn't used to this, wasn't used to Taylor or having to share her space with him. And she was beginning to think she never would be. Almost two weeks had passed since she'd found herself living in this converted fun house with a man she didn't remember. And—except for tiny flashes of thoughts she couldn't seem to catch hold of, couldn't unravel or examine—nothing was coming back to her about him or the life he claimed they'd had.

She remembered when she was in high school, her best friend's parents had gotten a rather unpleasant divorce. After the decree had been issued, Rhonda's mother cut out her father's face from every single family photograph she could find. It was like that for her now. Somehow her brain had cut Taylor Conway out of every single memory she possessed.

Was it motivated by talks of a divorce? she wondered. Was that what had somehow triggered this mental black hole?

Suddenly aware that he hadn't answered her, Taylor muttered, "Nothing."

"Taylor."

Something in her voice made him turn around, a pregnant note that told him she was about to follow up with something he should brace himself for. As if having to deal with a wife who didn't know you from the paper boy wasn't bad enough.

"Yeah?" he asked guardedly as he looked at her.

"Were we getting a divorce?"

"What?"

She took a breath and enunciated every word, as if she was seeking an answer from someone who was mentally impaired. "Were we getting a divorce, talking about a divorce, seeing a lawyer or maybe going to a marriage counselor?"

"No," he said emphatically. Then, in case Gayle was going to go over each of the sentence fragments bit by bit, he decided to make it perfectly clear. "No to all of the above." Taylor paused, looking at her face. Her expression remained the same. Puzzled. That made two of them. "Why?"

She shrugged slightly, one side of her peasant blouse slipping down off her shoulder. "I thought maybe something dramatic was the reason my mind shut you out of my life."

At least she wasn't balking anymore at the idea

that they were married, Taylor thought. That was something, right?

"No, no major storm in our lives," he told her for the umpteenth time as he pushed her drooping sleeve back up onto her shoulder. It would have taken very little for him to skim his fingertips over her skin, but he resisted the temptation. "Just a whole series of tiny ones." He offered a perfunctory smile, his lips quirking at the corners of his mouth before relaxing again. "Like always."

Gayle struggled to stifle a shiver. Her pulse had accelerated. Taylor's touch had seemed intimate, possessive. She didn't know why, but the slight gesture produced a wave of heat that traveled all through her. And although she was fiercely independent and guarded her space and her freedom zealously, in her heart of hearts, she felt a sort of deep-seated pleasure spilling throughout her body.

A second ago he was ready to go out the door and keep his silence. But her thought that they were considering a divorce had his defenses galvanizing.

"As a matter of fact," he told her, "today's the day I proposed to you."

She absorbed the words, trying to remember, to desperately summon up something that was in the vaguest way a memory. Nothing. "It is?"

He nodded. "September third."

The man she'd shared living space with for the past two weeks didn't strike her as the sensitive, sentimental type. More like the type who had trouble remembering when Christmas came each year.

She stared at him in disbelief. "You remember the day you proposed to me? Most guys don't remember things like that."

"Yeah, well, I'm not most guys." That was what he was trying to get across to her. That she'd shone on everyone else but said yes to him. That made him different from all the other men she'd ever gone out with.

Yesterday, in a moment of desperation, he'd placed a call to Dr. Sullivan. It had taken some doing, but he finally got to speak directly to the neurosurgeon. The doctor had told him that it wasn't unusual that she still didn't remember. He advised him to continue to be patient and to keep surrounding Gayle with familiar things.

The latter now prompted him to say, "Why don't we go to the restaurant where I proposed when I get back tonight? Maybe that'll trigger something for you." At this point, even though part of him had become resigned to the thought of winning Gayle all over again, he was willing to try just about anything to move the process along.

She caught her lip between her teeth, thinking. "What time?"

He saw a *but* coming and tried to head it off. "Any time you're free."

She flashed an apologetic smile. "That's just it, I'm not. I mean, I promised to attend this fund-raiser for the club where I used to train. It's tonight. I said yes weeks ago," she added.

The depth of his own patience surprised him as he asked evenly, "Do you have to stay for the whole event?"

She had planned to, but in light of what he'd just told her, she supposed she owed it to him to alter her agenda.

"No, I guess I could leave early. I could cite another engagement." Her mouth curved as she realized what she'd just said. "No pun intended."

"Make all the puns you want, as long as we get this straightened out sometime before I start collecting social security checks." He thought for a second. "I'll come with you to the fund-raiser. That way, you can spend a little more time at the party and then we can go to the restaurant from there."

She looked surprised at his suggestion. "But you don't like fund-raisers." The words had come out automatically, before she was even aware that they had occurred to her. Feeling uncomfortable, like being discovered with a smoking gun she wasn't aware of having picked up, she tacked on, "Do you?"

"How did you know that?" Trying to contain his excitement and not to jump to any conclusions, he still grabbed her shoulders. His eyes searched hers, looking for a sign, a clue. "Did you remember something?"

Gayle shrugged out of his hold and spread her hands before her helplessly. "It just came to me. Instinct, I guess." She looked up at him. "I don't know," she said honestly.

No one had ever accused Taylor of being an optimist. He didn't deserve the label by any stretch of the definition, but right now he clung to this small tidbit she'd unwittingly thrown his way.

It gave him hope.

He wanted to get going as it was getting late. Still, he lingered a moment longer. Looking at her a moment longer. Willing her to find her way out of this fog.

"What time do you have to be at the fund-raiser?" he asked.

"Six." Then, before he could ask her what she was doing about her nightly taping, she said, "I've got John covering for me at the station. John Alvarez," she added in case she'd taken too much for granted.

She kept treating him like a newcomer to her life and it irritated him. Irritated him because he knew her better than anyone, even her brothers.

"I know who Alvarez is. You're the one with amnesia," he reminded her, "not me."

"I just don't know how much you know about my world."

"It's *our* world," he told her tersely. "Bits and pieces might be separate, but it's *our* world, Gayle, yours and mine." Impatience filled him as he saw the odd expression on her face. He could almost see her retreating from him, erasing the tiny steps she'd taken forward. "What?" he snapped.

She lifted her chin defensively, balking at his tone. "You're making me feel claustrophobic."

A feeling of déjà vu passed over him, icy and chilling like the smoke created by dry ice. "You'll get over it," he promised her, then added, "you did the first time."

To his satisfaction, he saw her eyes widen. *Something else you can't remember,* he thought. They'd had this conversation once before, when she'd admitted that she did have feelings for him and that it worried her because she felt she was giving up pieces of herself. He'd answered by saying he didn't want pieces of her, he wanted all of her. Just as he was giving all of himself to her. Reconciling herself to that had taken Gayle time. But she had.

"Six," he repeated.

"Six."

"I'll be home by five," he told her as he finally made it across the threshold.

He wasn't home by five. Or five-fifteen, or five-thirty.

At 5:31, Taylor burst in through the front door, moving at the speed of a freight train with a full head of steam and doing his best to keep a frayed temper under wraps. Nothing more he hated than being late, even if an act of God *was* responsible.

And then he saw Gayle at the foot of the stairs. And stopped dead in his tracks.

She was wearing a floor-length, Kelly-green gown spun out of what looked like a shimmery spider's web. The all-but-translucent material adhered to her body like a second skin.

His palms suddenly itched. "I think I'm jealous of a bolt of cloth."

The look in his eyes as they washed over her stripped her of the impatient anger that had been building steadily with the passing of each minute. She tried to summon a little of it back. But her temper was brittle.

"Where were you?" she demanded. "I was about to leave."

The fund-raiser. Luigi's. His mind came back on-line. He made for the staircase.

"Three minutes," he tossed over his shoulder, stripping off his shirt as he ran up the stairs two at a time. "All I need is three minutes."

Gathering up the hem of her gown, Gayle followed him up the stairs. "I should have left ten minutes ago." She heard him opening the closet in her bedroom.

Their bedroom, she amended silently. His clothes were hanging on the right side of the walk-in closet she discovered he'd created for her. That she couldn't remember any of them was something she was getting accustomed to, even though it still chafed her.

"Where is this thing, anyway?" he asked.

She walked in just in time to see him kicking off

his shoes and then shucking his jeans. He wore no socks and seemed to favor briefs that were just that, brief.

Very.

Damn.

"Gayle?" he asked, looking up in her direction when she made no reply to his question.

She found out something just then. She found out that it was hard to answer when your tongue was suddenly sealed to the roof of your mouth because all traces of moisture had evaporated. Taylor's everyday clothes hadn't exactly been baggy, and his jeans had a nice way of adhering to his slim hips, but she had no idea that he had a body that would make art students and women under the age of ninety weep for joy.

Taylor's body was hard, muscular and taut, with a small waist and a butt she had a feeling she could bounce quarters off of. It made her want to go looking for her change purse.

"Newport," she managed to say, dragging her eyes away. Unfortunately she dragged them right to the wardrobe door, whose mirror reflected Taylor's image right back at her. It took a great deal of effort for her to form words. "It's in Newport Beach."

"You're the guest speaker, right?" he asked, dragging on his best pair of slacks.

He was aware that she was watching his every move, watching as the material slipped over his thighs and hips before he buttoned then zipped up the slacks. The look in her eyes pleased him. Again he told himself they were making progress. *Something* was going to make her come around to him. He just hoped he could hold out until it happened, because as things stood, angry or not, happy or not, all he wanted to do was take Gayle into his arms and make love with her. The hardest thing in the world was missing someone who was standing right in front of you.

It took effort for her to pull her thoughts together. They kept spilling out like peas that had been gathered up in an apron with a gaping hole in the bottom.

"What?" She blinked, focusing. The sentence he'd just uttered played back in her head. Something about a guest speaker. Her. She was the guest speaker. "Oh, right. Right," she repeated with feeling.

Reaching into the closet again, Taylor took out a long-sleeved light-blue shirt. Interpreting the look on her face correctly, he suppressed a grin. Barely.

Soon, he promised himself.

"Well, they're not going to start it without you, are they?"

She watched as his fingers worked their way down the front of his shirt, closing buttons as they went.

"No." The word came out as a sigh. Then, suddenly aware of the way that had sounded, Gayle cleared her throat and repeated "No" more forcefully.

Mercifully, he was covered again, she thought. Now all she had to do was block the image of an almost-naked Taylor out of her brain.

After quickly pulling on a pair of black socks to complement his gray slacks, Taylor grabbed a pair of newly polished black shoes and a navy-blue sports jacket.

"Ready," he declared. He nodded toward the bedroom doorway. "Go on, go."

She felt like she was being herded out of the room and down the stairs. Given her present state of mind, she really couldn't take umbrage over that. She was behaving like some dumb sheep.

"I'm assuming that you're going to drive," Taylor said as he followed her down the stairs. Reaching the last step, he dropped his shoes on the floor and stepped into them.

He shoved his arms through the sleeves of his jacket as she turned to look at him. She wanted to be angry, to get embroiled in an argument that would wind up creating some kind of fiery force field around her head. She had to extinguish the image that had branded itself into her brain.

With effort she did her best to pick a fight. "If you were going to be late, why didn't you call?" she demanded.

Leaning in front of her, he opened the front door before she had the chance. He stepped back and let her go first.

"I didn't know I was going to be late until I was

stuck in traffic." And it had been one hell of a traffic jam. A ten-minute drive turned out to be an endurance test for patience.

She gave him a quizzical look, not seeing the problem. "So?"

Her car was in the driveway. He'd parked his at the curb, to give her a wide berth. There were times when she didn't just turn corners, she took them. Literally. Clipping off edges of things as she passed.

Walking ahead of her, he reached the driver's side first and opened the door for her. "I couldn't call," he told her. "I had no phone."

For a second she'd thought he had changed his mind and was racing her for the driver's side. Feeling slightly foolish, she released a long breath, got in and buckled up as he closed the door for her.

She looked at him as he got in on his side. "Don't you own a cell phone?"

Taylor pulled his seat belt around, locking it into place. "Yeah. Forgot to charge it."

The only time he used a phone on a regular basis was to call the various suppliers he dealt with. Most of that could be accomplished before he went to work, since the places he called all opened early. He saw no reason to carry around a cell phone. As far as he was concerned, the shrill ring cutting into your life was a clear invasion of privacy. Gayle, on the other hand, lived by the phone. She had two of them in her purse, in case one died or malfunctioned.

"Sorry," he apologized again. "I wasn't counting on a three-car pileup happening on the freeway today."

She dismissed his apology with a wave of her hand before turning on the ignition.

"Doesn't matter now," she told him. With a quick, sudden jerk, she gunned the car out of the driveway and onto the street. "If we hurry, we can still make it on time."

And hurry they did. The whole way.

Because he was trying to win her over, Taylor didn't talk to her the way he normally might. Instead he did his best to hold his tongue. He tried not to look at the speedometer as she weaved from one lane to the next. She took advantage of every empty space, stuffing her sports car into it before changing lanes again.

When she took the downside of a hill as if she was piloting the first car of a roller coaster, Taylor just couldn't keep quiet any longer.

"You know, just because they put the number 120 on the speedometer doesn't mean that you should try to hit that speed."

She glanced at the rearview mirror to make sure no police vehicles were in the vicinity. She continued at her present speed. Traffic was fairly light and they were making great time.

Her eyes shifted to his for a split second. "I didn't take you for someone who exaggerated."

He pointed to the road, silently indicating he

wanted her to look there and not at him. "I'm not ex-
aggerating. Pilots on runways just before take off go
slower than you're going now."

She laughed at the comparison as she changed
lanes. "Afraid to die?"

His hand tightened on dashboard. From his van-
tage point, he gauged that she'd just avoided becoming one with the car that was now behind them, by
less than a fraction of an inch.

"No, I'm afraid of living mangled and having to
have an airbag surgically removed from my chest."

Biting off a choice word, Gayle nonetheless eased
the pressure she was exerting on the accelerator. The
speedometer gave up ten miles on the gauge. She
glanced toward it, then him. "Satisfied?"

"Getting there," he told her.

Did he want them to crawl? Keeping the retort
to herself, she eased up a little more on the accelerator. "Now?"

"Now," he told her with a smile.

Her attention lingered on the smile a shade too
long. The next second, looking back at the road
again, she exclaimed, "Damn."

Instantly alert, he looked for an accident about to
happen. To them. But there was no immediate danger of a collision in sight. He looked back at Gayle.
"What's the matter?"

She merged into the left lane. The sign ahead told
her that U-turns were forbidden. Just her luck. "I just
passed the turnoff."

Taylor didn't say anything. He was too busy trying to suppress the grin that so badly wanted to spread out over his features.

Chapter Eleven

Gayle didn't remember.

She didn't remember the restaurant when they finally managed to leave the fund-raiser at Luigi's in Newport Beach and make their way to it. Didn't remember the table for two by the window that looked out on the Pacific Ocean as beams of moonlight winked in and out along the surface of the dark waters.

Didn't remember him proposing to her.

Taylor found it difficult not to take it personally.

She remembered old movies, details about people she worked with, the ingredients in the one meal she could cook without having all the smoke alarms suddenly screech a warning.

But she didn't remember him.

Why?

The question echoed in Taylor's mind as they drove home, just as it had ricocheted through his mind over and over again ever since this whole surreal charade had started.

Taylor all but jammed his key into the front door, unlocking it. He was having a tough time controlling his disappointment. It had cloaked itself in anger, which he was trying very hard not to take out on her.

"I'm sorry," Gayle said quietly as she walked into the house just ahead of him.

She was subdued in comparison to earlier this evening. At the fund-raiser, she was bubblier than a newly opened bottle of champagne, talking to everyone who had come up to her. She worked the room like a pro, trying to secure more pledges for the club.

Even a club outranked him, Taylor had thought glumly.

At the restaurant, she'd been sunny, employing what he'd come to think of as her "public personality." It was something her father had ingrained in her. The public was never to see her as anything but upbeat.

But now as they entered the house, without the need to play to any audience, she'd suddenly turned quiet on him. It was as if someone had turned the volume down both on her voice and her personality.

She almost looked vulnerable, he thought. Almost but not quite.

"Sorry about what?" he asked, locking the door behind them.

Outside, the hot Santa Ana winds had descended from the desert less than half an hour ago and were whipping through the trees. The palm tree in the distance looked as if it was directing traffic, its fronds moving first one way, then another. The winds created a fierce noise not unlike the howling of a banshee.

Or a lost soul, he thought.

"Sorry that I didn't remember," she told him, dropping her purse on the side table by the door.

He paused for a moment, the strange note in her voice catching his attention. There was a look of sadness in her eyes, of regret. The lingering look of doubt he'd come across ever since he'd brought her to the hospital was gone.

He felt his way around carefully, knowing better than to take too much for granted when it came to Gayle. "Then you've stopped doubting that I'm your husband."

"Yes." She lifted her shoulders in a half shrug which was not nearly as careless as she pretended it was. "Actually, I started believing you a couple of days ago."

The only sound was the howl of the wind outside. Maybe he was opening up a fresh can of worms, but he had to ask.

"Why?"

Though she thrived on emotion, always had, there

were times when she gave way to logic. "Because nobody would go through this much trouble, stage photographs, get my brothers in on it, even the colonel, that kind of thing," she elaborated. "It has to be true." An enigmatic smile played on her lips for a moment before she added, "Even I'm not worth that much trouble."

He laughed shortly and shook his head. He was doing his best to keep this sense of hopelessness at bay. "Nice to know the accident didn't affect your ego, either."

She wasn't sure how he meant that, but she balked at any reference to having an ego. Nothing could be further from the truth. If anything, the person she was inside was insecure, not egotistical.

"That was meant as a joke," she told him.

Taylor sighed. He shed the sports jacket he detested wearing and dropped it onto the plastic covered sofa without a conscious thought as to what he was doing. "Yeah, I know." Pulling out his shirt from his slacks, he began to unbutton it. "Sorry, maybe I'm being a little testy."

"No more than usual."

Gayle picked up the jacket and brushed it off, something he noted that she always did whenever they returned from a function. She was doing it unconsciously. Naturally. Maybe some small part of her mind was staging a comeback. He tried not to get overly excited about what would have been, under normal circumstances, a very mundane act.

She saw him looking at her oddly. Had something fallen out of his pocket? She looked around and saw no reason for his expression. "What?"

"You're picking up my jacket."

She looked down at the material in her arms. "Well you left it on top of the plastic. Do you have any idea how dusty that must be with all the things you were doing here? You'll have to send it to the cleaners before it's completely clean again. Why are you looking at me that way?"

He allowed himself a smile. Inside hope had lit a candle. A large candle. "Because that's something a wife would do."

She had no idea why on the one hand she felt so attracted to this man and on the other, she had this desire to contradict everything he said. Was that what her marriage had been like? Constant skirmishes on the marital battlefield?

"Or someone who was trying to establish some kind of order in this land of chaos," she countered. Gayle thrust the jacket toward him. "Here, I'll even let you hang it up."

He took the jacket from her. "You can still nag, I see."

Gayle lifted her chin, all set to go a round or two with him. "I do not nag. I make tasteful suggestions."

Taylor rolled his eyes, then headed up the stairs. "Over and over again."

Scooping up the edge of her hem, she hurried

after him. "There's nothing wrong with reinforce-ment," she informed him.

Taylor's laugh was forced. "Is that what you call it, now?"

Under Gayle's watchful eye, he took the jacket over to the closet and hung it up. Then he removed his shoes, using the toe of one to work off the heel of another. His socks came off next. Then his shirt. He left both on a chair by the bureau.

Gayle couldn't draw her eyes away. Something stirred in the back of her mind, but as she tried to urge it forward, it remained in the shadows.

There was no denying that she was experiencing a very real sense of déjà vu. She'd stood like this be-fore, in some room, perhaps even this one, watch-ing him do exactly what he was doing.

But like a TV screen experiencing an invasion of annoyingly distracting lines and waves, the picture just refused to become clear no matter how much she willed it to.

When Taylor's long, tanned fingers went to undo the button at the top of his slacks, Gayle realized that she had caught her breath.

"What are you doing?"

"Avoiding another 'tactful' suggestion," he told her mildly. "If I take my pants off downstairs, you'll only complain about where I leave them. Besides—" he eased the slacks down from his hips, then hung them up, as well "—my cutoffs are here."

She felt a wave of warmth coming over her. Intense warmth. And there seemed to be a sudden shortage of air, not just in her lungs but in the immediate area around her. Gayle knew that she should have turned away. That standing like this, staring at him, was giving Taylor the satisfaction of getting the reaction she knew he was after.

But it was impossible to look away from a body like that.

Responses sprang forth inside of her own body like a fountain suddenly coming to life in the desert. Her mind might not remember this man, but there seemed to be no doubt that her body did.

Her tongue was resting in a chalky mouth.

"You sleep in cutoffs?" she heard herself asking. The words felt as if they were dribbling from her lips one at a time, like slow drops of water from a faucet.

"Sometimes," he told her, his eyes never leaving hers. "Sometimes I sleep in nothing at all."

Everything became exponentially hotter. Gayle could have sworn she was standing in an oven. The vague thought that the Santa Anas had somehow managed to sneak their way into the house, crossed her mind.

Taylor would have been responsible for that, too. The man had undoubtedly left holes in the structure where she couldn't see them.

Just like he'd created holes in her resolve to remember Taylor, really remember him before she allowed her other, more physical responses to take over.

She could feel her heart hammering in her throat. And her chest. How was that possible?

And why wasn't he putting something on that rock-hard body of his?

Her knees were growing weaker. "And which time is this?" Her voice was hardly above a whisper.

Taylor stood so close to her there wasn't even enough room to wedge in a prayer. Not one for strength. Or even one of thanksgiving.

"That's up to you," he told her.

She wanted some kind of outside power to come in and intervene. To take it out of her hands. She didn't want it to be up to her.

Because she wasn't strong enough to turn away.

His words seemed to shimmer before her, almost tangible enough for her to grasp in her hand. The next moment she was aware that she was grasping his shoulders. Standing in the high heels she still hadn't removed, the distance between point A and point B was not as great as it might have been. Point A were her lips, point B were his.

She wasn't completely sure just who cut away the remaining distance between them. It might have been Taylor, but she was fairly certain that she made the first move. That she was the one who brought her lips up to his.

The next thing she knew, she was being enveloped in his arms. He was pressing her to him. Pressing his mouth against hers. And even though she couldn't remember a physical relationship between them beyond the first time Taylor kissed her, something inside of her cried out for joy.

Like a flower sitting in darkness, suddenly exposed to the sun, her desire bloomed and took over.

Gayle surrendered to the inevitable not with resignation but a sense of elation that almost frightened her for its intensity. As far as she was concerned, she really still *did* not know him.

It didn't seem to matter. Her soul somehow knew him and that was enough.

She lost herself inside the kiss.

And then, suddenly, he was drawing back, away from her. "Gayle?"

It took her a moment to orient herself. Her insides were spinning, along with the room. She looked at his face, his expression, and knew what he was asking—whether she'd suddenly remembered.

Ever so slightly, she moved her head from side to side. She didn't remember. And right now she desperately wanted to.

"Make me remember, Taylor."

He didn't need anything more.

Sweeping her back into his arms, he kissed her over and over again, melting her.

Melting himself.

It was all he could do not to rip her gown off her body. But although in the past their lovemaking had at times gone way beyond the point of intensity, he knew that as far as she was concerned, this was the first time. Which meant that no matter what he wanted, he needed to go slowly. For her sake. For their sake.

So, though it cost him, Taylor held himself in check, moving ahead by increments. Making love to her with his mouth, with his hands, with every breath that left his body.

He drew her gown away from her slowly. His arms surrounding her, he found the zipper and moved it down along the curve of her back, until it came to rest at the base of her spine. He saw desire leap into her eyes.

His fingertips on both sides of the opened zipper, he drew the gown away from her as if he were peeling away an outer layer. The gown pooled at her feet, leaving her wearing a creamy white thong that seemed to be spun out of gauze and his fondest dreams. Her high heels and stockings that adhered themselves to the tops of her thighs completed the picture.

His heart in his throat, Taylor sank to his knees in front of her. Very slowly, he rolled first one stocking down the length of her leg, then the other.

Her hand on his shoulder, Gayle stepped out of each one at a time, leaving her shoes behind, as well.

And then, rather than rise to his feet again, Taylor brought his mouth down lightly along the areas that had for so long been his.

The heat of his breath found her. Making her crazy.

Gayle pressed her lips together to keep the deep,

guttural noise of pleasure from piercing the air. Her fingernails dug into his shoulder as she felt his assault on her resistance growing more intense.

Felt the heat traveling through her limbs. Through her loins.

He was doing things to her, things that all but made her leave her body behind and spiral off headlong into space.

She felt weak, ready to pool like hot lava at his feet.

Gayle bit her lip as the first climax came, rocking her. She was only half-aware of tugging on Taylor's shoulder, trying to get him to stand up. She wanted this to be a mutual experience, wanted to wrap her body around his. To feel every part of him against her and to have him feel her against him.

When he rose to his feet again, she saw herself reflected in his eyes. Felt a quickening throughout her body. Felt something she would have sworn was love, if only she was capable of it.

She blocked all thoughts from her mind.

And then, suddenly, they were together on the bed, her legs wrapped tightly around his torso, his body hot against hers. Their mouths sealed to each other's as wild sensations echoed and throbbed through her very core.

He possessed every inch of her.

By touch, by taste, all of her belonged to him. And she had never wanted anything so much in her life. Never felt anything like this before.

And yet, if Taylor was really her husband, she'd had to have felt this before.

Why? Why couldn't she remember?

And then all questions vanished into oblivion as she felt him shift his body over hers. Felt his hands join with hers as he drew them up over her head.

Felt the weight of his body as he began to move forward, into her.

Gayle raised her hips in response, urging him on, desperate to feel that final, all encompassing sensation she knew was out there, waiting for her. The joining occurred as she felt herself drowning in a sea of openmouthed kisses. She felt, too, an urgency to claim him for herself.

Her pulse escalated, beating erratically along with her heart as the tempo of their timeless dance increased, as she rushed to join him in the climb to the top of the mountain.

When the final burst consumed her, she cried out, enthralled in a kind of mindless ecstasy that, until this moment, she'd had no idea she was capable of. She wasn't alone in her reaction, she sensed, given the way Taylor had pushed himself farther into her.

Slowly, ever so slowly, the intensity abated, allowing them both to float back to earth, swaddled in a blanket of euphoria.

For one brief moment, she wanted this to be her last moment on earth. She wanted to be able to savor this moment and just withdraw from everything forever. Because this was perfect.

But it wasn't her last moment. And the world was there waiting for her when she finally opened her eyes again.

As was he.

Gayle knew that he was going to ask. A part of her was almost willing to lie, to give him the answer she knew he was waiting for.

But she couldn't lie. It wasn't her way.

Oh, no?

Gayle stiffened. What the hell was that supposed to mean? She felt as if she was going crazy. Why, why couldn't everything just come together for her? Why couldn't she remember a man who could make her body sing this way?

Why were these strange, formless doubts plaguing her?

Pivoting on his elbows, Taylor looked at his wife. He saw his answer on her face. He was fairly certain that if she'd just remembered, there would be a look of elation on her face, of triumph that she had met yet another challenge and had emerged victorious.

There would have been a look there other than the one he saw now.

With a sigh, he moved off her. Lying beside her, he gathered Gayle into his arms the way he always did after they made love. He did it then because neither one of them ever wanted the moment to end. He did it now because she was vulnerable.

As was he.

"You might not remember me," he told her, "but your body certainly does."

She was fairly certain another man would have thought that making the earth move for her was enough to jolt her memory back. Yet Taylor assumed nothing had changed.

She turned her face toward him. The closeness of his body made her feel safe even as she continued to be lost. "How did you know?"

"Saw the look on your face," he told her. "There was no sudden spark in your eyes, nothing that said your brain was back to normal and remembered me. You enjoyed yourself, but you enjoyed yourself with a stranger, not with the man you've been married to for the last eighteen months."

He was hurting, she thought, and she ached for him. But she ached for herself, as well. Because she was the one in prison and she had no way of knowing how long this jail sentence would continue.

Releasing her, Taylor sat up on the bed with his back to her.

She held her breath. Was he going to get up and go to bed downstairs? She didn't want him to leave her. To leave her here in this large four-poster bed with nothing but half shadows to keep her company. To taunt her.

He stood up, naked and as perfect as anything she'd even seen outside of a museum. She could feel her body quickening again, could feel the longing taking hold of her. Longing for him.

"Maybe it requires more than just once," she said quietly. He turned around to look at her. "Unless you're one of those men who just likes to do it once."

But even as she said it, she had evidence before her that Taylor definitely did *not* fall into that category.

He sat down on the bed again, facing her. "I'm one of those men who believes that something takes as long as it takes."

She didn't bother trying to keep the smile from her lips. "Which means twice?"

He lay down beside her, taking her into his arms. "Which means as many times as you want to do it."

And then, before she could ask him another question, Taylor was kissing her again. Kissing her as his hands began to roam over her body again, stroking her and burning away the desire to waste her breath on words when there were so many more worthwhile things to occupy her.

Chapter Twelve

Early-morning sunlight moved its way quietly into the room. Gayle stirred, squeezing her eyes shut to keep the intrusive light away.

As her brain shook off the last remnants of sleep, layers of last night returned to her. Her eyes flew open as the full impact of what had happened, what she'd done, sank in.

She'd surrendered last night.

Surrendered.

The word echoed in her brain, growing larger as she brought her surroundings into focus.

Surrendering meant allowing the man stirring beside her to have control over her.

No, damn it, it wasn't going to go that way. She'd worked too hard to maintain her independence just to throw it all away because some man was incredibly hot in bed.

She still had no idea what their relationship had been like before, she only had now to work with. And whatever happened now was going to undoubtedly dictate at least a portion of her future.

She was the master of her fate, not him.

Taylor stretched beside her as his eyes opened. He looked not unlike a cat who had fallen, face-first, into a vat of cream and had to drink his way out. "'Morning, Beautiful."

Gayle tugged the sheet around her, wishing she'd woken up earlier and been able to leave the scene of the crime. Or at the very least put on her clothes before he'd opened his eyes.

"'Morning," she replied crisply, her shoulders as stiff as her expression.

He knew that expression. She might not be able to remember their life together, but he was experiencing a very definite wave of déjà vu. Gayle had had that exact expression on her face the morning after the first time they'd made love together.

Disappointment touched him. He'd really hoped it would be different this time around. Apparently, you could take memories of the husband out of the girl, but the fighting core always remained.

Sitting up beside her, Taylor did his best to pretend that things were finally back on track between them. That this was just another average morning in their lives, no different from any of the others they'd experienced. It wasn't easy.

"It's still early," he commented, glancing at the clock sitting on his nightstand. "Want me to make breakfast?"

Gayle felt incredibly vulnerable and exposed. And desperate for a way not to appear to be either. The best defense was a good offense. She gave him a cold look. "Are you saying I can't cook?"

That hadn't been his intended message, but her question had a smile curving his lips despite the tension in the air.

"That really doesn't need saying, Gayle. It's more like a world opinion." He saw her look hardening. "Even you've admitted more than once that you can't."

All of her free hours when she was growing up had gone into training. Then there were all those tours. She'd never had time to learn how to cook and, frankly, no inclination, either. Her brothers teased her about it. But he couldn't.

Because she needed something to focus on, other than how much she'd given up last night, she let her anger flare. "How hard is it to make eggs and toast?"

His grin widened. "For the average person or for you?"

Hugging the sheet to her, she drew herself up as much as she was able. "And just how many breakfasts have you sampled over the years?"

He wasn't sure if she was using "breakfast" as

some kind of metaphor, but he was taking no chances. "Enough to know I didn't marry you for your cooking." Unable to help himself, he added, "Just like I didn't marry you for your even temper."

Her eyes narrowed. "And just what is it you did marry me for?"

He'd woken up in a damn good mood. Last night, he'd held on to the hope that maybe things were turning around again. For the positive. He should have known better. "Right about now I tend to forget." He caught his temper before it flared. "Look, I just wanted to do something nice for you."

Because of her mind-set, Gayle zeroed in on the one offending word. "I don't need you to 'do' anything for me."

About to retort, Taylor closed his mouth again. He was letting himself be sucked into an argument that was so less than pointless he couldn't even begin to unravel it.

He didn't have to. He'd taken this journey before. "Maybe not, but I know what you're doing."

She looked at him indignantly, still struggling to keep the sheet in place. "I'm not doing anything."

"Oh yes, you are," he countered. "You're scared so you're trying to push me away."

"Scared?" she demanded angrily.

"Yes," he repeated quietly. Firmly. Infuriatingly. "Scared."

Her eyes blazed as she glared at him. It took everything he had not to just pull her back into his arms and make love with her. Granted she was exasperating beyond words, but she was also magnificent like this.

"And just what the hell am I supposed to be scared of?" she asked. Her eyes narrowed into small, blue-green slits. "You?"

"Partly," he said, but he knew her well enough to know that he was just the catalyst here. "Mostly you're scared of you."

She laughed shortly, dismissing the idea as absurd. "I didn't notice a degree in psychiatry hanging off your toolbelt."

He didn't rise to the bait. She could send him over the brink with one word, but he was determined to be the sane one here. One of them had to be. And their marriage was at stake.

"Living with you has given me an honorary degree." With effort he attempted to reason with her. "Look, I'm not your father."

"What?" she growled out the single word. Taylor had just crossed a line.

Okay, maybe that didn't come out right, he silently conceded. But Taylor didn't know how else to proceed, except to just keep going.

"I don't want you to obey my every command, Gayle." The way they both knew her father had wanted. Still wanted, if she only let him. "I don't want to mold you or make you an extension of myself in any manner, shape or form. I just want you to be my wife."

"The little woman," she sneered, deliberately trying to set him off, because inside she felt as if she was losing. Losing to the look in his eyes, to the patience in his voice. She didn't want to lose. Because losing wasn't acceptable to her.

He merely shook his head. "Nobody in their right mind would ever think of you that way."

She glanced down, finding the insult in the words. Her body was outlined by the sheet that covered it. "Are you saying—"

"I'm saying that the way you said it was derogatory, and I've never thought of you in any other terms except that you are your own woman." His eyes held hers. "And that's just fine with me."

She pushed her way past the fears, the insecurities that had a way of surfacing unless she held them in check, and just looked at him for a long moment. "That's the way you think of me?"

"Yes." And then, because he knew she needed honesty, he added, "I've also thought of you as one hell of a royal pain in the butt, and right now, lady, you are going for an all-time record."

Stung, she reacted without thinking, her hand going back to gain momentum before she swung. Taylor caught her by the wrist, raising her hand above her head before she could make contact with his face.

The sheet she was keeping in place with her arms slipped and he became acutely aware of the fact that she had nothing on from the waist up. Or down.

Sleeping hormones all snapped to immediate attention.

Gayle turned him on now more than she had when they first came together as a couple. His eyes held hers, looking for the woman he loved more than life itself. "I don't want to fight."

A glint of triumph entered her eyes. "Afraid you'll lose?"

"Afraid I'll strangle you." He released her hand. "Damn it, Gayle, nobody has ever affected me the way you do." He looked at her long, slim throat. "I want to wrap my hands around that pretty little neck of yours and squeeze until all the annoying words are gone."

But that wasn't all, she thought. She could almost feel Taylor's unspoken thoughts gliding along her skin. "And?"

He took a breath. Until he'd fallen in love with Gayle, he'd kept his own counsel, kept his thoughts to himself. But now the idea of doing that seemed just too lonely. "And I want to make love to you until one or both of us expires."

She had no idea why a smile tugged at the edge of her lips. "So death is pretty much the bottom line."

"It usually is. As in 'till death do us part.'" And he'd never meant anything he'd ever said more in his life. He wanted to face forever with her. Not alone.

Raising the sheet back up around her again, Gayle blew out a breath. Some of the fight she'd felt was temporarily gone. She paused for a moment, then asked, "Where did we get married?"

The question came out of nowhere. Maybe it was a good sign. "In a hospital chapel."

She stared at him. Sunlight straining through blue- and amber-colored glass flashed through her mind. Something formless tried to pull itself together in her mind, but then it faded as she tried to grasp hold of it. The frustration was driving her crazy.

"Why a hospital chapel?"

He smiled. "That was your idea. You thought it was the best way to avoid the photographers. Except for the one Jake brought to capture the occasion."

"The wedding album," she remembered.

"Right. Your father and brothers were there, the first under duress." The colonel and he had a polite truce, which, according to what Jake had told him, was counted as a victory. The colonel didn't really tolerate too many people. "I think he felt I was marrying you for free swimming lessons."

"Knowing my father, he'd resent another man getting control over me." She glanced up suddenly, realizing what she'd said.

He laughed. "As your father, he should have known you better."

He was treating this with good humor. Maybe she'd overreacted, Gayle thought, then immediately upbraided herself. Of course she'd overreacted. Every time she gave a little of herself, she was afraid she'd never get it back. Training with her father had done that to her. She wondered if she would ever get over that.

Gayle pressed her lips together, then forced out an apology. "I'm sorry about before."

"I was expecting it." He saw the puzzled look cross her face. "You did it before." And then, because only one of them remembered, he explained, "The first time we made love. You went from being a sultry summer breeze to a class-five hurricane in about as much time as it took to say it."

"And you rode it out."

He shrugged. "Had to."

She searched his face, trying to understand. The man was good-looking and an incredible lover. He could easily have had anyone he wanted—on his own terms. Why had he stuck it out with her? "Why?"

Didn't she know? On some deep, inner level, didn't she know how he felt about her? How he would always feel about her? "Why do you think?"

"You have a death wish."

He laughed then, and the sound enveloped her like a warm comforter on a cold, crisp winter morning.

"My wishes don't involve death in any form." He threaded his fingers through her hair, moving it away from her face. "They do involve you, however. You're the best game in town. In any town."

Was that it? Was she just a game to him, a challenge, or was there more to it than that? Her readiness to take offense, to pull away had deserted her. "I don't think I understand."

He smiled into her eyes. As gorgeous as she was, it was her eyes he loved best about her.

"You don't have to. At times, neither do I." Because he still wasn't certain of her reactions, he resisted the temptation to draw her back into his arms the way he sorely wanted to. "But so far what we have between us works." He sighed, remembering. "Or *was* working until you took Sam up on his dare. He didn't mean it, you know. Didn't mean for you to dive into the ocean from that point on the boat."

She shook her head, not remembering the incident. But she did remember something inherent about herself. Something that she was certain had its initial foundation in the fact that she was her father's daughter. "I can't walk away from a dare."

He knew that, but it still didn't make any sense to him. It never had. "Why? You don't have anything to prove."

She smiled, more at the words than at him. "Maybe you don't know me as well as you claim."

"Let me revise that, you don't have anything you *need* to prove. You're an Olympic gold medalist, a successful sportscaster. You're young, beautiful and you have a sexy husband. The tabloids even approve of you. Of us, as a matter of fact." He found that pretty amazing, given the vulturelike tendencies of that quarter of the press. "Everything is perfect."

She pursed her lips together. "Except that I don't remember you."

"Except that you don't remember me." His gaze searched Gayle's face. Hoping. "Not even a little?"

"There are moments," she allowed. Moments that raised her hopes, only to dash them in the next heartbeat. "Tiny shards will flash through my brain, only to disappear, leaving nothing illuminated in their wake. So, on the whole, no."

He should be used to disappointment by now, he thought. But he wasn't. So he shrugged at her words, doing his best to appear philosophical. He wasn't much good at pretending, but he tried for her sake. Because, despite her earlier bluster, he felt she was coming around. Not remembering him, but accepting him as part of her life. And not balking at it.

"It's still early. The doctor said it might take time."

"He also said it might never come back," she reminded him. She tried not to allow the thought to depress her. But she did find the thought the most frustrating of all, that the life she'd had with Taylor up until this point might remain a secret from her, locked in her brain for the rest of her life.

He made light of the suggestion. "That's called covering all bases. Doctors all do that. But he saw no reason for us not to be optimistic that this is just a temporary condition. Most of the time, the amnesia *is* temporary."

"But most of the time," she countered, "the amnesia is all-inclusive."

He wasn't going to go there, wasn't going to allow himself to dwell on dark thoughts. He could do that about a lot of things, but not when it came to her.

Taylor took hold of her shoulders, making her look at him. "Every case is different, Gayle. And you are going to remember me."

His eyes held hers. He wouldn't lie to her, she thought. "You're sure?"

"I'm sure."

She wanted to ask him how he knew, how he could be so certain about something about which she had such grave doubts. But in her heart she had a feeling that Taylor wouldn't be able to answer her question in any manner that would be satisfactory to her. So she quietly clung to his words as if they were a promise. Because she needed to.

She smiled at him, feeling something other than just desire stir within her. "You know, you can be very nice at times."

This time he gave in to himself and slipped his arm around her. To his relief, she didn't pull back. He felt her hair tickle his shoulder. "I can be very nice all the time."

She looked up at him. "So why aren't you?"

He brushed his lips against hers so lightly she thought she imagined it. "It would be too boring."

This time the stirring she felt was definitely desire. "Does that offer for breakfast still stand?"

"Sure." He brushed his lips against hers again, this time a bit harder and with more feeling. His arms closed around her. "In a minute."

"A minute?" Her eyes laughed at him. "You want to do it that fast?"

He kissed her again. And again. And in between he murmured, "Okay, five minutes."

She threaded her arms around his neck, her body pressing against his. "Make it ten."

He was already drawing her back down on the bed. "Whatever you want."

She frowned at the man who had initially hired her. Finished with the latest set of promos she'd promised to tape, she was on her way out of the studio, planning the evening that lay ahead. She wasn't sure just what that entailed, but ultimately she intended for them to wind up in bed together.

Her plans were placed on hold when the news producer called her into his office. One look at his face and she had an unnerving feeling that her plans were about to be changed.

When he opened his mouth and told her the assignment, she knew it. Still, she heard herself repeating, "You want me to go out of town?"

Will Carroll nodded, joining his hands together and resting them on his considerable bulk. "Just overnight." It was obvious by his expression that he'd thought she'd be pleased and was now mystified himself. "What's wrong? You love going on the road, and this is just a quick stop. Just like the last trip," he reminded her. "Into Phoenix and then back home again." He looked particularly happy with himself as he added, "I've even booked the same room for you."

The same room.

Gayle looked at her producer blankly. Something else she didn't remember, she realized, and held her frustration at bay. No one at the station knew anything about her accident or her memory lapse when it came to her marital condition, and she wasn't about to fill anyone in. So she merely nodded at Carroll's words.

In an odd way, she felt the tiniest bit heartened. Apparently there was something besides Taylor that she'd forgotten. She knew that at the very least, this might make Taylor feel better.

Damn it, she didn't like this, didn't like not remembering. People were comprised of their memories, and she wanted hers back.

She realized that Will was looking at her oddly. "Something wrong?"

She shook her head. "No, just trying to rearrange a few things in my head to accommodate the trip, that's all."

The producer picked up a rectangular envelope with two boarding passes peering out of the top, one for Phoenix, one for a return flight.

"Well, don't spend too much time rearranging. The flight's at three. Game starts at seven."

She didn't bother pointing out that she already knew when tonight's game was starting. Instead, she took the tickets from him and resigned herself to postponing her night of passion until tomorrow. She had a game to cover. "Okay."

The scent of flowers filled the interior of his car. As did the off-tune melody he was whistling.

The music stopped when he saw that her car wasn't in the driveway.

That was all right, he just got home before her. She was probably working late at the station, taping promos or an extra segment. He could wait.

When he let himself into the house, he saw the blinking light on the telephone answering machine. A feeling in his gut told him that he was being too optimistic.

It figured. With Gayle, there was always at least one step back for every two steps forward.

Putting the bouquet of daisies down on the counter, he pressed the play button on the answering machine. A second later he heard her voice.

"Taylor, I have to cover the Angels-Diamondback game in Phoenix. I'll be back tomorrow. I'm really sorry about this."

He frowned at the machine as her voice faded. An annoying beep told him that the message was over.

"Not as sorry as I am," he said aloud.

Picking up the bouquet, he was tempted to deposit it into the garbage. He told himself he was overreact-

ing and picking up bad habits from Gayle. So instead
he crossed to the cabinet farthest from the refrigerator and got out the vase she kept there. He poured a
little water into the vase and stuffed in the bouquet,
not bothering to take off the plastic wrapped around
it.

"The best-laid plans of mice and men," he muttered under his breath.

It looked as if he was going to be spending the
night alone.

He knew he could probably get together with one
or both of her brothers, but he didn't much feel like
being around people tonight. He'd been counting on
spending time with Gayle, on wearing her down a
little more.

With a sigh, he looked around the room. He supposed he could work on the living room. There was
nothing stopping him, but right now, he didn't feel
up to that, either.

He noticed the stack of mail on the breakfast bar.
At least two days' worth. Gayle got around to it
about once a week. With nothing else to do, he decided to look through the mail, see if any bills
needed paying before they became overdue.

Sorting, he divided the mail into three piles. Her
mail; his and the mail they received jointly, which
usually amounted to catalogs and ads.

When he came across the hospital bill addressed
to Gayle, he stopped and whistled softly. Talk about
speed. He thought it took about a month to process

a hospital bill. Obviously Blair Memorial wanted its money as fast as possible.

They both carried insurance. Hers was through the station, his was through an individual carrier. He imagined that hers would cover the charges completely, since an accident had been involved.

He might as well get the process going, he thought as he opened the envelope.

The logo on top of the bill proclaimed it to be for out-patient services rendered a month ago in Phoenix General.

Chapter Thirteen

The eerie feeling of déjà vu shimmied along Gayle's spine her the moment she crossed the threshold and walked into the hotel suite the station had reserved for her.

She couldn't remember being here. Yet she had to have been. Where else could this feeling be coming from? Besides, Will had said he'd booked the same suite for her. So she had to have been here before.

It didn't come back to her.

And yet…

Gayle was hardly aware of putting money into the bellman's hand as she looked around the room, searching for something to trigger her memory. But when he said something to her about how nice it was to see her again, Gayle looked at the young man sharply.

"You've seen me here before?"

"Yes, ma'am." He put her overnight case on the bed. "I was the bellman who brought your bag up the last time." And then he flashed her an overly toothy grin. "I guess with all the traveling you do, it's hard for you to remember one person."

No, that wasn't the case. She prided herself on remembering everyone she came in contact with, not just the celebrities.

Frustration took a bite out of her. Before the accident, she had complete recall, about people, places, events. Now, it was as if she was a length of fabric that moths had attacked, chewing away one complete section.

Except now it looked as if there was more than just one section missing.

She looked around again as the bellman crossed to the window. There was nothing she could recall about being here. And yet, this uncomfortable feeling that she *had* been here before haunted her. Something was trying to get through, but all the doors and windows were locked, blocking its access.

"When was that?" she pressed. She needed to draw up some kind of a timeline. Maybe that would help her zero in on what else she forgot besides Taylor.

The bellman didn't even have to pause to think. "Just last month, ma'am." About to open the drapes, he looked down at the bill she'd just pressed into his hand. "You were very generous the last time, too." Tugging, he pulled open the drapes. Harsh sunlight immediately filled the room. "And you look a lot better now, if you don't mind my saying so."

"Better?" What a strange thing for him to say. Gayle looked at his name tag. "What do you mean by 'better,' Wyatt?"

He seemed pleased that she bothered to use his name. It made things somehow more personal between them. "You were real pale the last time, like you were coming down with something or just getting over it. Sorry," he said suddenly, apparently realizing that he'd gone a little too far into the personal realm. "My girlfriend says I talk too much. I'll get out of your way now." And with that, the bellman known as Wyatt closed the door behind him and left.

Standing in the middle of the room, Gayle slowly looked around at her surroundings. It was a perfectly lovely hotel suite. What was it about it that made her feel so uncomfortable? What was she feeling that her mind wouldn't let in?

Will had said that he—or at least his secretary who makes all the arrangements—had gotten her the same room as before, as if it was something that she'd wanted. But if it was, why did she have this odd anxiety strumming through her? As if she was waiting for something to happen.

Had something happened in here that her mind hadn't wanted to deal with? And did it have anything to do with Taylor?

God, she wished she knew.

Momentarily defeated, Gayle sank down on the bed beside her overnight case and covered her face with her hands. Was she ever going to figure this out? Was she ever going to remember any of it, much less everything?

She absolutely hated dealing with the mental gap. She'd always been the type to want to know everything: answers to every question she came across, the bottom line to rumors, everything. And now the biggest mystery she had ever encountered in her life had to do with her and she hadn't a clue.

With an exasperated sigh, Gayle glanced at her watch. It was already after six. She had a game to attend.

Maybe when she came back, her memory would be clearer and some minute detail might come back to her.

At least she could hope.

Opening her overnight bag, she took out her somewhat outdated PDA, a recorder in case she had any thoughts about *anything* on the way to the stadium and a trusty pen and pad in the event she had any random thoughts regarding the interview she was to conduct.

For a woman walking through a fog, she congratulated herself for being pretty together.

* * *

Taylor stared at the two sheets of paper before him, one a summary, one an itemized statement for everything that had been pressed into use during Gayle's short outpatient stay at Phoenix General. Still hoping that maybe he was seeing things that weren't there, he picked up the rectangular envelope and looked at the upper left-hand corner of the envelope. The return address was marked Phoenix General.

Was it some kind of a mistake? A foul-up in the hospital billing department? Things like that happened far more frequently than the general public was aware of.

Chances of that were slim, he thought grimly. Both the summary and the itemized versions had her name on them. Gayle Elliott Conway. He frowned to himself. At least they got that part of it right. Maybe they got the rest of it right, too.

But if this was her bill, if Gayle had gone to the hospital while she was out of town covering a game, why hadn't she said anything to him? Either at the time or when she got back?

And what the hell did this code mean, anyway?

He was staring at the bottom of the itemized statement, in the area which had the letters DX embossed on it. Following that, which he knew stood for diagnosis, was a mysterious collection of letters, followed by numbers.

ICDA-8. What was that, anyway? He had no clue,

only that it was somehow tied in to whatever had prompted Gayle to seek medical attention.

Damn it, everything was shorthand these days.

Taylor looked at the mysterious group of numbers. He had a feeling that trapped inside those numbers was the reason behind why Gayle had gone to the hospital for emergency treatment.

What the hell could they stand for?

Muttering under his breath, Taylor made his way across plastic sheeting and drop cloths down the hall to the room that they had both agreed would serve as their joint office once it was completed.

The smell of fresh paint still lingered. He'd finished painting this room the day before the accident. That morning, before they left for the dock, they'd moved the furniture back in. There were two mahogany desks in the room, each facing away from the other.

That had been Gayle's idea. She'd said if she was facing him, she'd never get any work done.

A fond smile lingered on his lips for a moment. She'd said that back when she'd known him, he thought ruefully. Back when they both had trouble keeping their hands off each other, especially when the other claimed to have work to do.

Last night and this morning, he'd thought maybe the old Gayle was coming back. But it was the "old Gayle" who had kept this from him.

For all he knew, that might even be the reason behind this whole thing. Maybe it was an elaborate charade after all, to draw his attention away from whatever it was that involved this hospital visit.

A grim expression creased his face.

Maybe Gayle had been growing away from him even before this accident. It was obvious that she was keeping secrets from him. Significant secrets. Because if this was just a matter of a sinus infection or some minor complaint that had gotten out of hand, he thought, looking at the papers in his hand, she would have told him about it. This happened a little more than a week before her accident. Before she conveniently "forgot" him.

She would have been capable of talking to him about the reason for the visit.

Unless it was something she was trying to keep from him.

His expression was grimmer than ever as he turned on his computer and waited for it to warm up. Maybe he could find out on the Internet what the strange code numbers meant. His initial response would have been to call the hospital's billing department, but it was after six and they were probably closed.

If he didn't find what he wanted on the Internet, he'd have no choice but to call the hospital tomorrow. That meant waiting until morning.

He felt antsy already.

When the phone beside his computer rang, he was so completely lost in his search for the meaning behind the "ICDA-8" code that it took a second for the sound and its significance to register.

He was in no mood to be civil.

Yanking up the receiver, he fairly barked out a "Yes?" into the mouthpiece.

"Taylor? Is that you?"

Her voice, like smooth, warming whiskey, curled into his system. But his feeling of betrayal, of bewilderment was hard to work through. It was all he could do not to let the bitterness out.

"Yes, it's me." There was more than a little background noise behind her. He had to concentrate to hear her voice.

"Are you all right, Taylor?" she asked. "You sound strange."

For once I have a reason, he thought, staring at the two offending pages on his desk. "According to you, I'm a stranger, so sounding strange would be normal." He heard her pause on the other end. Before he could wonder if that was the end of it, and the beginning of the end of them, she pressed on.

"What's wrong, Taylor?"

Nothing, I hope. Everything, probably. But this wasn't something they could talk about on the phone. And, to be completely fair to her, he wasn't sure just what it was they *were* actually talking about, other than her lack of trust.

Maybe it was nothing and she didn't want to worry him. He knew how independent she was. It was a good excuse, but somehow, it rang hollow for him.

"Nothing," he finally said, lying. "I just don't like knocking around in this big house without you."

"Speaking of 'knocking,' from what I saw, you like knocking things down in that big house. Why don't you go and eliminate another wall?"

He felt as if all his energy had been siphoned away. "I don't feel like working."

She attributed that to her sudden disappearing act. She knew he'd planned to come home early in order to spend time with her. After last night, she was looking forward to it herself. No one was as disappointed about this as she was.

"I know what you mean. I'm sorry about this, Tay, I really am. But this came up at the last minute and I had no choice."

Before they'd gotten married, he'd made her a promise that he would never interfere with her work. He knew she needed to work, needed to be exactly who and what she was. But what about the other promises, promises they'd both made? Like never to lie to each other. Or to keep secrets.

He struggled to keep his temper under control. "It's your job."

He'd fairly growled out the words to her. "You don't sound very convincing," she said.

Taylor blew out a breath as he dragged a hand through his hair. "Yeah, well, I had a long day."

And then, instead of hanging up or just continuing to exchange small talk, she blew him away by saying, "I miss you."

The noise behind her was growing louder. She was probably calling him from the game she was supposed to be covering, he guessed. The din partially blotted out what she'd just said. Taylor was sure he'd misheard her. "What?"

Gayle raised her voice. "I said I miss you," she repeated. "I've got to stay in Phoenix overnight, because by the time the game's over and I do my interview, it'll be late and you'll already be in bed, so there's no point in catching a red-eye flight." He heard another noise, closer this time, near the vicinity of the cell phone. He envisioned Gayle cupping her hand around the mouthpiece as she said, "I wish I was there with you."

He wished he could believe her. But now he didn't know if he could *ever* believe her again. "Yeah, me, too."

He heard her laugh and tried not to let the sound into his system. "Someone is going to have to do something about the romantic way you talk, Taylor. You just sweet-talk a girl right off her feet."

Taylor frowned at the teasing tone. He was in no mood to let her wrap him around her little finger. "I'm a doer not a talker."

He could almost hear the grin in her voice as Gayle replied, "Amen to that. Look, I'll be back tomorrow before noon. Can you knock off early tomorrow? I'd like to make it up to you."

Her sultry voice when she said the last sentence caused his imagination to take flight. He struggled to strap it down. "What about work?"

If she noticed his cool tone, she gave no indication. "Will's letting me tape the scores early and then the station can just run the tape in the proper segment for the rest of the evening."

"What about late scores?"

"Nothing that I can't handle," she assured him. "This time of year, the teams are down to a significant few games. There are only a couple of baseball games a day and as for the other sports, they can have John sub for me." She hesitated before taking her next plunge. Since he was her husband, she was jumping with a safety net in place. "Keep the bed warm for me, Tay."

He thought of last night and a smile crept out, despite the negative thoughts plaguing him. "No need, you'll heat it up plenty yourself once you get here."

Her laugh, soft and low, echoed in his head long after she'd hung up.

He looked back at the offending pages he'd brought into the room with him.

Maybe it was all just a big misunderstanding. Maybe he was letting himself get worked up for no reason because of the unstable situation he was in. Maybe he was creating all these dark scenarios when it was all perfectly innocent.

Doggedly he went back to searching through the Internet, looking to demystify the code numbers. He found a site that dealt with medical diagnoses that corresponded to the various ICDA-8 code numbers. He discovered that not only was there something called ICDA-8, but ICDA by itself, as well. Taylor snorted, uttering a few ripe words under his breath. Until just now, he hadn't even been aware that there was one set of code numbers, much less two.

The world was getting too damn complicated.

Which was why he'd opted to work with his hands when it came to forging a career for himself. Working with his hands, creating something out of nothing the way he did, gave him some sense of control.

Except that right now he hadn't a clue as to how to settle down his out-of-control life.

An infinite number of codes corresponded to an equal number of diagnoses. He kept on scrolling, going through what seemed like an endless stream of numbers, numbers augmented by decimal increments.

After a while, he felt as if he was going cross-eyed, but there was no other option available to him. He had to continue looking for the code numbers imprinted on Gayle's hospital statement.

Finally, nearly half an hour later, he found the right numbers.

When he did, he wished he hadn't.

The diagnosis that corresponded with the ICDA-8 numbers cut through him like a dull-edged knife, taking out huge chunks of his soul.

Taylor double-checked the numbers on the page, marking them with his index finger as he looked back up on the screen.

But no matter now many times he looked back

and forth, the numbers didn't change. They remained the same. The diagnosis remained the same.

The pit of his stomach twisted, making him feel ill.

When he could feel his legs again, Taylor stood up and went to Gayle's desk. He began opening drawers, rifling through them until he located her address book. Because he had insisted on it, she'd written down the numbers that were important to her in longhand, putting them in an old-fashioned address book. He said he'd only use it in case of an emergency.

This constituted an emergency.

When he'd made his request for an address book that he could hold in his hand and page through, she'd called him a hopeless throwback, but there'd been affection in her voice.

He couldn't help wondering now just how much of that had been genuine, and how much of it had been faked. Because if the page he was looking at was true, and there was no reason for him to believe it wasn't, then she couldn't love him. Not if she'd done this without telling him about it.

Damn it, he was her husband. He had a right to know this kind of thing.

An ugly reason reared its head as to why she'd deliberately kept him in the dark, but Taylor refused to entertain it, refused to even recognize it. Because if he did, then he knew it was the beginning of the end for them. For him.

Accepting the reason would signal the death knell of their marriage far more effectively and quickly than her selective memory loss. He could ride that out. He didn't think he could ride out discovering that she'd been unfaithful to him.

Maybe he was even being a fool about that, he thought. Maybe she didn't even *have* a memory loss. Maybe all that was just her way of creating a diversion.

Anger filled in all the available vacant spots inside him.

He finally found her address book under a pile of computer printouts she'd shoved into her bottom drawer. He flipped through the pages, looking for one phone number in particular.

When he found it, he called the number, only to be put through to an answering service.

"No," he snapped after the woman was finished with the prerehearsed statement. "I do not want to leave a message. This is Taylor Conway and I need to talk to the doctor as soon as possible. It's about my wife, Gayle Conway." He stopped, realizing that he had no idea which name Gayle used at the doctor's office. "Gayle Elliott Conway. This an emergency," he added.

The woman's voice filled with sympathy. "What kind of emergency?"

"I'd rather tell the doctor," he answered curtly.

It was clear that the woman on the other end didn't know whether to believe him or not. Uttering a sigh, she promised to see what she could do. And then the line went dead.

As dead as Taylor felt inside.

He dropped the receiver back into the cradle and continued sitting where he was. Staring at the hospital bill and the code numbers that represented the diagnosis he didn't want to accept.

Fragments of conversations he'd had with Gayle, both before she'd left for Phoenix the last time and after she'd returned, played themselves over in his head. She knew how he felt.

How could she have done this? For *any* reason?

Chapter Fourteen

A long sigh of relief escaped Gayle's lips the moment she slid in behind the wheel of her sportscar and buckled up.

Finally!

After putting her key into the ignition, she turned on the engine and backed out of her designated space in the TV studio's parking lot. The past twenty-four hours had been interminable, at least three times longer than a normal day.

The previous night's tossing and turning hadn't exactly helped matters. Ordinarily she could drop off the second her head hit the pillow if she was tired. Strange hotel rooms and unfamiliar sleeping accommodations had never troubled her. Because of all the meets she'd competed in around the country and the world, that was the norm for her. Over the years she'd become accustomed to sleeping anywhere at any given time. She'd been known to be refreshed after taking a catnap in an airport.

But this hotel room had been different. There was more here than just the furniture. A presence of some kind.

"The Ghost of Christmas Past, right?" she mocked herself aloud.

Except that it really wasn't all that funny. Some "thing" had been there in that room, waiting for her to discover it. Waiting for her to remember.

Like being there before, she thought cryptically. That was just the problem, she *still* couldn't remember being there, yet by all accounts she had been. There was no reason for that bellman to lie about seeing her there before, or for Will to make up a story about booking the same room for her. What had happened in that suite that was bothering her so much now?

She'd kept a pattern all night, falling partially asleep, only to think that there were people in her room, crowding around her bed, talking, sometimes to her, sometimes to each other. And all the while, amid the noise, there were all these bright lights shining down on her.

Wry amusement had Gayle shaking her head as she turned the car toward the road that eventually fed into her development. If she told that part to anyone, about feeling as if there were people in her room, prodding at her beneath bright lights, they'd probably think she was babbling about being the subject of an alien abduction.

Damn, but she felt drained now. After her unsettling night, she'd come into the news studio almost completely exhausted.

Thank God for makeup, she thought. The makeup girl at the station murmured something about the dark circles under her eyes looking like tire tracks. Julia had asked her if she'd partied with the team after the Angels had shut out the Diamondbacks, scoring seven to nothing. To avoid any further speculation on Julia's part, she'd said yes.

The truth was that after her interview with the Angels' newest relief pitcher, and despite an invitation from the team's manager to go to the party, she'd opted to return to her hotel suite. All she wanted to do was pack her things and go to bed. She'd thought she was going to get a full night's sleep so she'd be fresh and rested this morning.

Instead she looked like something the cat had debated dragging in and then passed on.

Gayle pushed thoughts of her princess-and-the-pea type night out of her mind and concentrated on the present. She was almost home.

She smiled. She'd started to think of that drafty, hulking structure—which looked as if it was straight out of something that would have enticed the Addams Family—as home. She was making progress in the right direction.

God knew she was eager to see Taylor. She still didn't remember being his wife, but she was beginning to understand why she had married the man in the first place. And why she would do it again, if it should ever come to that. Her initial reactions to him—this time around—she qualified, had all but faded into the background. She was beginning to unravel the veiled reasons behind her behavior. Things were finally starting to fall into place for her.

What she must have done the first time around was to finally get out of her own way. Which meant that she'd made up her mind to stop being suspicious of Taylor.

Not that she would have felt he was after her money or trying to carve out a piece of the limelight for himself because he was marrying a celebrity. She'd only had to spend a minimum of time around the man to realize that thoughts like that never entered Taylor's mind. Those suspicions belonged to her father. The colonel had never thought any man was capable of wanting her for herself, only for what she could do for him. He'd drummed that into her head over and over again, almost as much as he'd drilled her about swimming techniques. He always said she had to be careful because there were men who wanted to take advantage of her.

Had she not had her unique personality, Gayle was fairly confident that the colonel would have caused some very serious, albeit completely unintentional, damage to her self-esteem.

However it was the concern the colonel didn't voice out loud that had been the primary deterrent to her forming any long, lasting relationships. Her father didn't want her involved with a man because he didn't want any other man exercising control over her.

There, at least, they were in semiagreement, Gayle thought. She didn't want any man thinking he could tell her what to do, either. So even the smallest hint of that had her moving in the opposite direction. If her path crossed that of any strong male, she was instantly on her guard, wary of any undue influence.

And yet, men who gave in to her, men she could steamroll over, didn't hold her interest for any length of time. They bored her. There was no chemistry, no spark. It seemed, from all indications, that she was doomed not to have any kind of meaningful relationship with any men other than her brothers.

Gayle smiled to herself. She supposed that gave her something in common with Kate, the shrew in Shakespeare's play. And while she didn't view herself as being tamed by Taylor, like the heroine within the play's play she only gave that impression when the occasion suited her. In a way it was a variation of the old saying, "You get more flies with honey than with vinegar."

And Taylor Conway was definitely a honey, if a

somewhat stoic one, she thought. He was a man of integrity who wanted no free tickets in life, no free rides. He paid his own way. His pride demanded it. You had to respect a man like that. That he also set the sheets on fire was an added bonus.

Despite the fact that she'd left the studio bone tired, Gayle could still feel her body quickening as she turned down a familiar street. Less than half a mile to go.

She mentally crossed her fingers that Taylor's dark green truck was in the driveway.

After her flight got in at John Wayne Airport, she'd taken a cab to the studio, sat in on the editing of her interview with the relief pitcher, done her score highlights for the afternoon and early evening shows, and left the rest of it all up to the station's other sportscaster, John Alvarez. Everything had been accomplished at almost fast-forward speed. She couldn't wait to get home.

Taking a sharp turn to the right, she pulled up into the driveway.

She was home.

And so was he, she thought in triumph as she looked at his truck. The engine was still making those soft, popping, cool-down noises, so Taylor must have just gotten here himself.

Gayle could feel her body priming. Anticipating.

Getting out of the car, she didn't even bother to take out her overnight bag. It would keep. All she intended to be wearing tonight was Taylor.

Unlocking the front door, she called out, "Taylor, I'm home."

The words had a familiar ring to them. She'd done this before, called out his name as she'd entered the house. Maybe the night she'd spent in the eerie hotel suite was indirectly making things come back to her. She certainly hoped so.

"Taylor?" she called again when there was no answer. "Where are you?"

Standing right inside the doorway, she could see into three of the rooms. The truck was in the driveway and there were lights on in the house. He had to be here.

Taylor felt his entire body tense at the sound of her voice.

He'd been waiting for her to come home ever since last night. Over the past twenty-four hours, he'd run the gamut of emotions, going from furious to confused to heartbroken and back again in no particular order but with almost breathtaking speed.

Emotions still ran through him, moving like crazed rabbits fleeing an oncoming predator. And blanketing them was this overwhelming sense of betrayal. He had loved this woman and lived with her for more than a year and a half and apparently didn't know her at all. Because the Gayle he thought he knew wouldn't have done this. At least, not without talking to him first.

He'd finally gotten through to her doctor last

night, but when he'd asked his question, the woman had cited doctor-patient confidentiality. She couldn't tell him anything. Her hands were tied, she'd said.

There'd been sympathy in the doctor's voice, but he didn't want sympathy; he wanted answers. And by not saying anything to him, Dr. Roberts wound up confirming his suspicions just the same. Because if what he'd asked her about Gayle had been off base, she would have said as much. Doctors were freer to comment on wrong guesses than on correct ones because in that case it would be giving nothing away.

When he'd hung up, barely murmuring goodbye, he felt as if his soul had suddenly become ground zero for an all-consuming forest fire. Everything, *everything* felt dead inside.

He'd gone to work, forced himself to go through the motions, hoping to somehow find a way to deal with this sense of betrayal. To somehow find a way to forgive Gayle.

In his heart, because he loved her, he knew he would have forgiven her anything. If only she'd come to him. But she hadn't. And then the accident had wiped him out of her mind. What did that say? That he was less than nothing to her? That all there was between them was fantastic sex and nothing more?

It wasn't enough, not for him.

His body felt like lead now as he walked toward the front of the house. Toward her. The woman he no longer knew.

"Taylor?" Gayle called out again, beginning to get worried. Where was he? She didn't hear any pulsating noise, so he wasn't running any tools that could be blocking out the sound of her voice.

After tossing her purse onto the table, her keys landing on top, she started toward the stairs. Maybe he was in their bedroom and didn't hear her.

But then she saw him coming toward her from the rear of the house. She could feel the smile blossoming on her face, feel it from the inside as well as on her lips. She hadn't realized until this second how much she'd really missed him.

How much she was looking forward to tonight.

"There you are." She moved toward him, her arms out. All she wanted to do was hug him and be hugged by him. "I was beginning to think you wanted to play hide-and-seek."

"No," he told her, his voice deadly still. "I don't want to play at all."

She stopped just short of touching Taylor. Her arms dropped to her sides as she stared at him. From out of nowhere, fear came galloping up on a black charger, its hooves beating an erratic tattoo in her chest. Every nerve in her body tightened.

She could almost feel the skin on her scalp tingling. In a very bad way.

Gayle searched his face for a clue and found none. Only that he was shutting her out. Why? She'd been away for only one day, what had gone on here in that time?

Her head began to ache.

"Taylor?" she said slowly, trying desperately to smile, to tell herself that everything was all right. "What's wrong? What happened?"

His eyes were frosted as they looked at her. "You tell me."

Like someone trapped in the throes of an ongoing nightmare, Gayle shook her head in what felt like slow motion. She didn't know how much more of this confusion she could take.

Was this some kind of psychological game he was playing with her? Had she just dropped her guard only to fall for someone who was emotionally abusive?

No, he wasn't like that. She would have bet her life on that. There *had* to be some kind of logical explanation why he'd gone from Dr. Jekyll to Mr. Hyde.

"I don't know what you mean." She tried to soften her voice, to sound as if she wasn't worried, only curious. "Taylor, what's going on?"

Maybe he should just walk out now, before his temper erupted. Before he shouted at her, demanding to know how she could have just thoughtlessly thrown away a life like this.

But he didn't go. He stayed there, right where he was. Maybe, against all odds and reason, there was a tiny shred of him that hoped she could still save the situation. Still make it right somehow by giving him a reason that made sense. Though he couldn't see his way clear as to what that reason could be.

Struggling to keep everything bottled up, Taylor pulled out the bill he'd stuffed into his back pocket, shook it open and held it out to her. "Does this look familiar to you?"

Gayle stared at the sheet blankly, but made no move to take it in her hand. Afraid that if she did it would cause something awful to happen.

What was it he was accusing her of? And why had he convicted her without a trial? She raised her chin defiantly. Anything she had felt for him only moments ago iced over.

"No," she answered crisply. "Why should it?"

"Let me give you a hint." He watched her face, waiting for a crack in her veneer. She was good, he thought. She was acting as if she didn't know what he was talking about. But she did. Too many things fell together for this to be some kind of gross mistake. "It's a bill. From the hospital."

Why was he carrying on about that? It didn't make any sense. "So Blair Memorial mailed the bill to us instead of sending it to the insurance company. So what? These things probably happen a lot."

"Not Blair Memorial," he corrected, pointing to the top of the page where the hospital's address was written. "Phoenix General."

"Phoenix General?" she echoed incredulously. What was he talking about? "I never went to Phoenix General." But even as she made the denial, some nebulous feeling uncoiled in her brain. She resisted, inwardly afraid even as she retained her bravado. "There has to be some mistake."

If she only knew how much he wished he could believe that. But it was too late. He'd verified the bill this morning by calling the billing department at Phoenix General.

"No mistake, Gayle, you were there." He saw the confusion in her eyes. *Give it up, Gayle. I found you out. Found out your secret.* "They've got all your information right. Your name, your birthday, our address." He indicated each line as he spoke. "The timing is right, too. It was while you were there on the last road trip with the Angels."

She stared at the sheet like someone in a trance. "I don't remember."

Because his heart was still breaking, he shouted at her. "Gayle, that's getting old. You remember everything, but me—and now this. It's too convenient, don't you think?"

Gayle grabbed the page from him, almost tearing it. She scanned it quickly, but her brain was under siege. It took her several seconds to separate the lines and focus on the individual charges.

What jumped out at her was that there was a charge for the use of the emergency room and for outpatient surgical supplies.

She'd had surgery performed on her.

Gayle looked up at him, a helplessness pulling her under for the third time. Nothing was making sense. "This is like a nightmare. I swear I don't— What are these numbers?" Suddenly seeing them, she pointed to the digits that came after "Dx."

He took a breath, afraid his voice would crack. "That's your diagnosis."

He sounded so odd, so distant. She'd never heard him like this. Something inside of her scrambled for high ground, for safety. But there was none. She searched for anger to draw on, but even that was deserting her. "What does it say I had?"

His eyes narrowed. He hated this. They were supposed to be a couple, a team of two, not opponents. But she had done that to them.

"Don't play dumb, Gayle."

Something inside of her broke. "I am *not* playing dumb," she shouted at him. "Don't you think I'd say something if I could remember?" And then she stopped abruptly as an idea came to her. They were supposed to have had an open relationship. "Didn't I tell you why I went to the hospital E.R. when I came back from the road trip?"

Was she toying with him now? Was that it? Taylor found that he really had to struggle to hold on to his temper. He felt almost mortally wounded.

"No, you didn't say a word about it. You just came home from the trip and acted as if it was business as usual. You just looked a little pale around the edges," he recalled. "Maybe the strain of keeping secrets from me was wearing on you."

"I didn't—" She began to shout a protest that she didn't keep secrets from him, that she didn't know if she had any secrets to keep, but the word suddenly began to echo in her brain. "Secrets," she repeated, not looking at him.

Secrets.

She realized that the word had somehow been part of her semidream, as well.

Did she have secrets from him? If she did, they were secrets from her now, as well.

"Yes, secrets." His mouth twisted into a grim expression. "A pretty sterile word for what you did." And then his temper, his hurt, finally erupted. "Damn it, Gayle, why didn't you come to me before you did it? Why did you just shut me out this way?"

"What way?" she cried in exasperation. "What is it that you think I did?"

How could she pretend not to know? You just didn't forget something like this, like a missed item in a grocery cart. "You killed our baby."

Her face turned completely pale as she stared at him. "What?"

"This code," he jabbed at the line with his index finger, "it stands for termination of pregnancy. That was our baby you just swept out of your life. You didn't even think enough of it, *of me,* to let me know you were going to do it."

He pressed his lips together, trying to get under control. Remembering. They'd sat right there, on the sofa, with her dangling her bare feet over one upholstered arm, talking about the future. And he'd actually felt bad, telling her they were going to have to put on hold for a while having kids. God, he'd been such a fool.

"You even had me going with that talk about wanting a family." He looked at her accusingly. "What was that, your decoy plan?"

The room had suddenly gotten very hot. And air in her lungs had vanished somehow. She found it was hard to focus.

"I didn't have a decoy plan. I don't know anything about this." Sweat began forming along her upper lip, her lids, her hair line. Slipping down her spine. "I...didn't..."

Gayle couldn't finish, couldn't push any more words out of her mouth. She was too weak. She started to sway. Her knees felt as if they'd been dissolved, and she didn't have the strength to stand up anymore.

"Gayle?"

She heard a voice. Taylor's?

It was coming to her from a long distance away, as if whoever talking was standing on the other end of a long tunnel.

She couldn't see who it was.

Someone was grabbing her hand. Holding her upright. Even with support she couldn't stand. Everything was spinning.

The room was shrinking, its edges rapidly becoming outlined in black. What light there was around her was disappearing.

She tried to scream for help, but the cry became

caught in her throat. The darkness swiftly devoured it before a sound could emerge.

And then the darkness came to claim her.

Chapter Fifteen

Taylor managed to catch her in his arms before she hit the floor.

"Gayle? Gayle?"

Leaning against him limply, Gayle didn't respond to the sound of his voice. Fear materialized in his chest, growing stronger by the second.

His pulse racing, Taylor's first thought was to call 911. But then he thought she might be better off if he took her to the emergency room himself.

Torn, he looked down at Gayle's face. She looked so pale, so frail. He was afraid that she'd had a relapse, or that maybe the doctor, despite all the fancy scans at Blair, had still managed to miss something. What if she had a tumor or a blood clot forming?

Damn it, why had he yelled at her like that?

Still holding Gayle in his arms, he forced himself to take a deep breath and calm down. He had to think logically.

Maybe she'd just fainted.

Women fainted, right? he thought, silently asking himself the rhetorical question. No woman he'd ever known, certainly not Gayle, but he knew it did happen. Maybe it had happened to Gayle.

He was having trouble thinking straight. At this moment everything seemed completely pulled inside out, upside down and thrown into another, not quite parallel, universe.

He looked at her again. She was breathing evenly. More evenly than he was, he thought. He felt on the verge of hyperventilating.

"I used to be calm before you," he told the unconscious woman.

Rather than rush to the telephone or to the hospital, he told himself to play it by ear. Picking her up in his arms, Taylor carried his wife over to the sofa, yanking away the plastic as he balanced her against his body. He used one leg propped up against the coffee table to keep her in place. With a section cleared away, he then laid her down, praying he wasn't making a grave mistake by not summoning help.

She still looked paler than snow, but her pulse felt stronger. That had to be a good sign. Right?

Her eyes remained closed.

"Damn it, Gayle, you're tying me all up in knots.

What's going on with you? With us?" he whispered, as he gently pushed the hair away from her face.

A compress. She needed a compress.

Taylor hurried to the kitchen. After tearing off two paper towels from the roll, he doubled them up to form a rectangle, then dampened them. Once he was back in the living room, he placed the dripping towels on Gayle's forehead.

Her eyelashes fluttered. After a moment she stirred. When she finally opened her eyes, Taylor felt as if he'd just been given a stay of execution. It didn't matter what she'd done, what secrets she'd kept from him, he'd deal with it. *They'd* deal with it. Nothing mattered except that Gayle was in his life, mercurial, unpredictable, but his. And well.

Feeling slightly bewildered, Gayle tried to sit up. He gently pushed her back down onto the sofa. "Stay down."

This is where I came in, she thought.

The thought came and went, making no sense to her. She took a shaky breath, feeling completely out of focus. Her head was killing her and there was something wet and clammy on her forehead.

"What happened?"

Her voice sounded so reedy, Taylor thought, as doubts continued to plague him. Maybe he should take her to the hospital. He wasn't qualified to make judgments about her health.

"You passed out." Again she tried to sit up and he pressed his hand to her shoulder, pushing her down and trying to keep her still. "I said stay down. I don't want you passing out again."

A very real feeling of déjà vu took hold, refusing to release her. He'd pushed her down like this before, told her not to sit up before. Not that long ago.

"Fainting," she corrected weakly. She fought to keep her eyes open and the room from spinning again. "Drunks pass out, I fainted."

The contrary statement brought a thin smile to his lips. Now *that* sounded like his Gayle. "And you're back." Taking her hand, he sat down beside her, claiming just the edge of the sofa.

When she tried to remove the makeshift compress from her forehead, he caught her wrist, stopping her. It was like dealing with a little kid, he thought. An impatient, contrary little kid.

God, but he loved every contrary bone in her body.

"It's dripping," she protested when he caught her other hand to prevent her from snatching away the wet towels. The excess moisture had worked its way down her cheeks and hair and continued on a jagged path. "My shoulders are getting wet."

With a resigned sigh, Taylor removed the compress and dropped it on top of the plastic-covered coffee table.

"You look a little bit better," he told her. "You've worked your way from Casper the Friendly Ghost and you're up to Snow White." It was meant to amuse her. Instead, he saw her eyes suddenly widened. He couldn't read her expression. Braced for anything—he hoped—he asked, "What's the matter?"

Her heart slammed into her rib cage. She grasped his hand. "I remember."

He told himself to be cautious, not to get his hopes up. "Remember what? Why you went to the hospital in Phoenix?"

As soon as he said it, a deep-rooted chill passed over her. The hospital. Oh, God, the hospital. She fought to keep the sob out of her voice. To keep a sense of horror at bay.

"Yes," she said quietly. "That. And you."

Still he didn't want to jump to the conclusion he ached to embrace. Disappointment would be too overwhelming if he was wrong. "Remember me how?"

"In every way."

Memories came flooding back to her in no particular order, with no distinct rhyme or reason. It was as if she was standing in front of a dam and not just the floodgates but the very dam walls had broken. The water came rushing at her, threatening to wash her out to sea.

Her fingers tightened on his hand, as if that would somehow help her brace herself.

Panic filled her voice. "Taylor."

He slipped his arm around her. "I'm here, honey, I'm here." Even as he said it, he saw that she had started to cry. It was remorse, he thought. Remorse for what she'd done. Any anger he'd felt at the deed, at being shut out, all disappeared. He just wanted her to be all right again. "Maybe I'd better get you to the hospital."

"No, no more hospitals. Please," she begged. That was what her weird dreams had been about in the hotel room, she realized suddenly. She wasn't dreaming; she was remembering. Remembering being in the operating room. They'd only given her a local, but everything had become unclear during the procedure.

She held on to Taylor, feeling hollow. "I lost our baby."

"I know," he told her softly. Holding her close to him, he did his best to comfort her.

Gayle drew back, shaking her head. She knew what he thought. And he was wrong.

"No, no, you don't," she cried. "You don't understand. I *lost* it. My body aborted it. It was a miscarriage. I started bleeding in the hotel room and I drove myself over to the hospital. I got there just in time to be too late. The baby was gone." Her mouth twisted in self-mockery. "I thought I was so damn healthy." When she looked at him, there was a bottomless sadness in her eyes. "I haven't been sick a day in my life since the second grade." It didn't make any sense to her. "But I couldn't keep the baby."

Her words replayed themselves in his head. "You miscarried?" Taylor could only stare at her. "You didn't go in for an abortion?"

Everything inside of her scrambled together, braced. Ready to mount a defensive. How could he think that about her?

"No!" she cried.

"Then why didn't you tell me?" It didn't matter if it didn't make any sense. What mattered was that Gayle had gone through all this alone, he thought. He should have been there for her. "Why didn't you tell me you lost the baby?" Another question quickly occurred to him in the wake of his first. "Why didn't you tell me you were pregnant? And how could you be pregnant? You're on the pill."

She lifted her shoulders in a shrug she felt too drained to even complete. She'd asked her gynecologist the same question.

"Dr. Roberts said these things happen. Chances are small, but they do happen."

So the doctor had known, he thought. She probably knew about the miscarriage, as well. He struggled not to feel like an outsider in his own life. "I still don't understand, Gayle. Why didn't you tell me you were pregnant?"

Emotions welled up in her. Trying to keep a tight rein on herself, she hadn't allowed herself to mourn properly. She banked down tears now. Tears wouldn't help. "I tried."

Was she having another memory lapse, he wondered. "When?"

"That conversation I had with you about having kids." She could see by his expression he needed a few minutes to recall it. "That was supposed to be my way of segueing into telling you." Supposed to be, she thought. Except that it had turned sour on her. "But then you were so firm about waiting, about not wanting any kids until you felt you could provide for them yourself." She closed her eyes, remembering his exact words. "You said there was nothing wrong in waiting and that right now you were perfectly happy with it being just the two of us."

A sadness entered her eyes as she looked at him again. "I tried to get you to change your mind by saying that maybe by the time you felt you were ready, I wouldn't be able to get pregnant. That the longer you wait to get pregnant, sometimes the harder it is."

Now he was beginning to understand, or at least to see it from her perspective. His own words came back to haunt him. "And I said that if it was never more than just the two of us, that would be okay with me." He realized now how that had to have sounded to her. "I said that for you, Gayle."

Maybe her brain was still foggy. She didn't understand. "For me?"

"In case things didn't go the way we planned when we were ready. I didn't want you to feel that you *had* to give me a baby." He felt so helpless now, thinking of what she'd gone through. First believing he didn't want the baby she was carrying, then carrying the overwhelming sadness of the miscarriage by herself. "You should have told me, you know. You shouldn't have had to face that by yourself."

She knew that now. But at the time she'd felt emotionally estranged from him, believing he didn't want the baby in the first place. "I thought you'd be upset that I was pregnant. And then when I lost the baby, I was afraid that you'd be relieved that our life wasn't going to change. I couldn't have stood that," she told him. "It was easier just not telling you."

How had signals gotten so confused between them? It felt as though misunderstanding had just built on misunderstanding. And then he thought of the way he'd wrapped himself up in his anger and accused her of having an abortion behind his back.

A rueful expression played on his lips. "I'm sorry I went off like that. But when I saw that the code numbers meant 'termination of pregnancy'—"

He'd jumped to a conclusion, she thought.

"You assumed that I had an abortion." She looked at him, wondering if either one knew the other at all. "How could you have thought that, knowing how I feel about kids?"

Taylor dragged a hand through his hair. She was right. He should have known better. Should have known she wasn't capable of that, certainly not without telling him first. But after everything that had happened, part of him had felt as if he didn't know anything at all.

"It hasn't exactly been a normal few weeks," he said. "I felt cut out of your life because life with me was the only thing you couldn't remember. And then to find out that you were keeping things from me—"

"I thought you didn't want the baby," she repeated. "And when I lost it, I was really afraid you'd say something like, 'it was for the best' and then I'd wind up hating you. I just couldn't risk something like that happening." She splayed her hand over her flat belly. Fresh tears rose to her eyes, threatening to spill out. "I guess in my mind I felt it was all so awful. When the accident happened, my brain seized the opportunity to wipe it all out of my mind." She looked at him. "Including the father of my baby."

He forced a smile to his lips. "I guess that's as good an explanation as any." The doctor had told him there were no easy solutions, nothing they could hold on to as gospel when it came to things like amnesia. He was just damn relieved that it was all behind them.

Taylor gathered her to him again. Part of him felt reluctant to ever let her go again. He knew that, given her independent streak, saying as much would probably go over like a lead balloon. So he just held her and was grateful.

"Sure you don't want to go to the hospital to get checked out?" he asked several minutes later.

She moved her head back and forth against his chest in reply before she gave voice to her sentiments. "No, I've had enough of hospitals for a while." And then she raised her face to his. "But I wouldn't mind if you wanted to play doctor and check me out."

Instead of agreeing, the way she'd expected him to, she saw Taylor frown as he looked at her. "Are you sure you're up to that?"

More than up to it, she thought. She *needed* it. Needed to feel for a moment that there was nothing else in this world but pleasure. "Don't treat me like a fragile doll, Taylor. It's all I've been thinking about since yesterday morning after you left for work."

He looked at her in surprise. "What, making love with me?"

She nodded. "That, and coming home to you." She smiled at the sound of that. Home. This falling-apart building she found herself living in with Taylor was home. Taylor was home.

He had missed seeing her smile—that smile of self-deprecation that only he got to see. "I guess I fell faster for you the second time around," she said.

Yes! something inside of him cheered. Outwardly he tried to remain the picture of calmness. "Practice makes perfect."

Well, that wasn't exactly what she'd thought she'd hear. "How about you?" she prodded.

He looked at her with an innocent expression. "How about me what?"

"Why did you stick around?" She realized she meant the question seriously. Another man would have said a few choice words and left, wife or no wife. Yet he had stuck it out. "I was pretty horrible there for a while."

There wasn't even a hint of a smile on his lips as he deadpanned. "And this would be different from your normal behavior how?" Immediately Taylor hardened his muscles, knowing what was coming. The next second, Gayle's doubled-up fist made contact with his biceps. Hard.

The blow actually stung. Apparently, she hadn't lost any of her strength during this ordeal. "Hey, I thought you were supposed to be weak," Taylor protested. "That hurt."

She grinned. God, but it felt good to be back. Good to banter with him. To think of him as her soul mate. Her friend as well as her lover. "Must be my superwoman strength returning."

He didn't return her banter. Instead he looked at Gayle for a long moment, searching her face, still worried about what he might find there. But his Gayle was back. The old Gayle. The one he'd pledged before God and a handful of people to always remain faithful to.

"So, you remember?" he finally said.

She beamed at him, so very relieved to finally be out of the fog. To be able to look at Taylor and remember him beyond the moment she'd opened her eyes on the deck of the boat. "I remember."

"Everything?" he prodded carefully.

She placed her hand in the middle of his chest, delighting in the soft, rhythmic sound his heart was making. His heart belonged to her more than her own did.

She raised her hand as if she was taking a pledge. "Every last sexy bit," she swore. She dropped her hand to her lap as she continued. "Right down to the fact that I married a really terrific guy who sticks by me no matter how loopy I get."

He didn't want to waste time talking about himself. That only embarrassed him. He was far more interested in securing a promise from her.

"No more secrets?"

"No more secrets, Taylor," she said seriously. "That goes for you, too, you know."

"I know." It hit him that he had come perilously close to losing her, not just once but twice. And the first way would have left him alone with so many questions.

She could almost feel him thinking. Could almost feel his eyes as they glided along her skin. "What?"

Instead of answering immediately, he surprised her by kissing her forehead. Leaning back, Taylor pulled her onto his lap and laced his fingers together around her shoulders. "I love you."

He didn't say that often. Actually, he hardly ever said it at all. She'd heard the words from him perhaps two, maybe three times in all the time they'd been together, while she said it so often, she'd lost count.

It made his declaration very, very special.

"I love you, too, Taylor."

Taylor shifted her weight, then slipped his hands

beneath her legs and back and rose with her in his arms. Feeling almost giddy, Gayle wrapped her arms around his neck.

"Let the games begin," she laughed.

"No, no games," he told her.

She sobered. Had she misinterpreted the signs again? "You're not just going to put me to bed, are you?"

His mouth formed a hint of a smile. "That's part of the plan."

Something about the way he said it caused her to silence the protest on her lips. Feeling heartened, yet without anything tangible to hang it on, she asked, "What's the other part?"

"I thought maybe we could get started making a baby," he told her lightly.

A baby. He was serious. She could see it in his eyes. She felt like cheering. And then she remembered. "But I'm back on the pill." And lightning just didn't strike twice in the same place.

He nodded, taking it in stride. "You can stop as of tomorrow," he told her as he began to walk with her toward the stairs. A teasing note entered his voice. "Just think of tonight as a dress rehearsal."

"*Dress* rehearsal?" she repeated, looking at him uncertainly.

"Clothing optional," he corrected. Taylor paused to brush his lips against hers just before he took the first step up.

She grinned as she looked up into his eyes. "My favorite condition."

When Taylor kissed his wife, it was a long time before he took the next step.

* * * * *

0107/23a

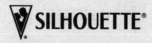 **SILHOUETTE®**

SPECIAL EDITION™

A MONTANA HOMECOMING
by Allison Leigh

When Laurel Runyan came home, finding her first love, Sheriff Shane Golightly, as a neighbour was a surprise. Was Laurel ready to give her home town—and Shane—a second chance?

THE BABY DEAL
by Victoria Pade
Family Business

For Delia McRay, hooking up with Chicago playboy Andrew Hanson on a Tahitian beach was a fantasy come true. But when Hanson Media met with Delia's company months later to land her account, there was a pregnant pause…

LUKE'S PROPOSAL
by Lois Faye Dyer
The McClouds

When Rachel Kerrigan sought Lucas McCloud's help to save her family's ranch, he thought of their fleeting youthful kiss and agreed. It was strictly business and the old family feud wouldn't matter…

Don't miss out!
On sale from 19th January 2007

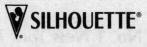

♦ SILHOUETTE®

0107/23b

SPECIAL EDITION™

THEIR SECRET SON by Judy Duarte

Bayside Bachelors

The beach-blond son of stunning socialite Kristin
Reynolds had to be his—because, once upon a time,
fireman Joe Davenport and Kristin had been lovers.
Joe could handle parenthood without reigniting the old
flame!

DANCING IN THE MOONLIGHT
by RaeAnne Thayne

The Dalton Brothers

Dr Jake Dalton's life was in tumult, thanks to the
return of childhood crush Magdalena Cruz, a US Army
Reserves nurse injured in Afghanistan. Would Jake's
offer to help Maggie make her realise what she'd been
missing?

THE LAST TIME I SAW VENICE
by Vivienne Wallington

For Annabel Hanson and Simon Pacino, Venice was the
beautiful city where they'd fallen head over heels in love.
Now, determined to reignite the still-smouldering embers
of their relationship, Simon pursues his estranged wife to
the city that brought them together…

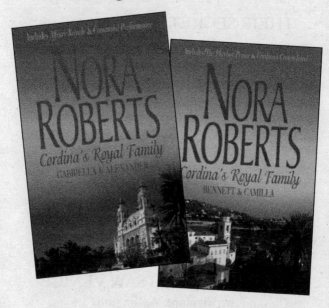

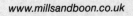

4 FREE

BOOKS AND A SURPRISE GIFT!

We would like to take this opportunity to thank you for reading this Silhouette® book by offering you the chance to take FOUR more specially selected titles from the Special Edition™ series absolutely FREE! We're also making this offer to introduce you to the benefits of the Mills & Boon® Reader Service™—

- ★ FREE home delivery
- ★ FREE gifts and competitions
- ★ FREE monthly Newsletter
- ★ Exclusive Reader Service offers
- ★ Books available before they're in the shops

Accepting these FREE books and gift places you under no obligation to buy, you may cancel at any time, even after receiving your free shipment. Simply complete your details below and return the entire page to the address below. You don't even need a stamp!

YES! Please send me 4 free Special Edition books and a surprise gift. I understand that unless you hear from me, I will receive 6 superb new titles every month for just £3.10 each, postage and packing free. I am under no obligation to purchase any books and may cancel my subscription at any time. The free books and gift will be mine to keep in any case.

E7ZED

Ms/Mrs/Miss/Mr ....Initials ....

BLOCK CAPITALS PLEASE

Surname ....

Address ....

....

....Postcode..

Send this whole page to:
UK: FREEPOST CN81, Croydon, CR9 3WZ

Offer valid in UK only and is not available to current Mills & Boon® Reader Service™ subscribers to this series. Overseas and Eire please write for details. We reserve the right to refuse an application and applicants must be aged 18 years or over. Only one application per household. Terms and prices subject to change without notice. Offer expires 30th March 2007. As a result of this application, you may receive offers from Harlequin Mills & Boon and other carefully selected companies. If you would prefer not to share in this opportunity please write to The Data Manager, PO Box 676, Richmond, TW9 1WU.

Silhouette® is a registered trademark and under licence.
Special Edition™ is being used as a trademark.
The Mills & Boon® Reader Service™ is being used as a trademark.